Judgment Day

Judgment Day

& the God.SED

John

ISBN: Softcover 978-1-4535-9063-8

This book was printed in the United States of America.

To order additional copies of this book, contact:
Xlibris Corporation
1-888-795-4274
www.Xlibris.com
Orders@Xlibris.com
88153

Dedicated to God,

The Holy Jesus Christ and to my beloved Mother

INTRODUCTION

Hi! to all the good readers, the story which you are about to read is about the truth which has been forgotten by many people around the world, by writing this story I wanted to remind every single person in the whole world that we have not been sent to the Earth without any purpose or without any reason, I wanted to remind people that we will be judged for the deeds we did, we are doing and the deeds which we will do in future. It is good to rethink that what would really happen to any one of us if the end of the world would come soon,

This story is about a couple whose names are John Seven and Sara Thomson, and their love, faith and believes which were tested by God during the beginning and the end of the Judgment Day. I have taken the truth from The Holy Bible and explored them by adding some ingredients in it so that it would not only be able to touch your hearts and souls, but also entertain and make you feel enjoyed by reading my book.

I hope, I will be able to send you back on the track which leads to the hands of our creator, the one for whom the impossible is possible, without whom we would be nothing and would never exist. Enjoy the ride. May God bless us all Amen!

THE NEW HEAVEN & THE NEW EARTH

There were many beautiful white clouds in the Sky; the Earth was covered by colorful Flowers and Trees which were covered by blossoms. The holy city was placed at the middle of the kingdom, its appearance was never been seen by anyone before as it looked like the rare Jewel, clear as a crystal, there was a great wall around the city, which had twelve gates, each gate was made by a single pearl which were being protected and guarded by Twelve Angels, there were twelve names on the gates which were the Twelve Holy tribes of the sons of the Israel which were always open for all the blessed creatures whose names were written in the Book of the Holy son to enter inside of it, there were three gates at its East side, there at its North side, three at its South side and also there at its West side. From the wall of the city, Twelve Fountains were flowing out on which the names of the Twelve Apostles of the Holy son were written. The city lied foursquare; its length was as same as its width, its length was about 2220000m, and its walls length was about 6480cm, the wall was made by the precious Jewels of Jasper while the city was itself made by purest Gold as well as its streets, they were as clear as glass. The foundation of the city was too made by several precious Jewels such as Jasper, Sapphire, Agate, Emerald, Onyx, Carnelian, Chrysolite, Beryl, Topaz, Chrysoprase, Jacinth, and Amethyst.

The city didn't have any Temple for worshiping as its Temple was God and his Holy son there was no need of the light of the Sun or Moon as the city was brighten by the glory of the God and his Holy son, there was no more darkness in any side of the kingdom .

At the other side, the River of life was flowing out from the throne of God and of his Holy son, through the middle of the street of the city, there was also a green and large tree of life standing at its other side with its twelve fruits hanging from it, the leaves of the tree were used for healing the destructed nations, there was no existence of any sorrow, pain, fear, injustice and violence as the God and Holy son has entered the earth and made peace in throughout the land, for then people could see Gods face and as his true believers were worshiping him, as the world was now smiling and happiness was everywhere.

On one side, Thousands of angels were designing the wall and the gates and constructing the city, and on the other, there were many female angels, laughing, singing, and preparing the feast, on the other side, male angels were practicing, and developing their Holy skills, on the other side young angels were sitting all together and listening to the stories about human beings and the way they lived on earth and the works they had done, they were learning about humans cultures, traditions, behaviors, their faithfulness, the power of their love and so many other things. Some young angels were also asking questions about the story of Adam & Eve, so the whole earth was involved in developments and perfect duties.

There was a beautiful peace in the land, every creatures looked very happy and joyful as they were being protected and loved by their maker. Even the animals never looked happier than those days, everything was simply perfect, the feeling of sadness was vanished forever. All the angels from different colors and races were working together as one and there was no existence of corruption, discrimination, and injustice among any one of them as they were now the members of a same family and had a single leader to lead them all.

There was a huge crowd sitting near the River of Life, they were all listening to John Seven as he was telling them his life story and the way he fought with Evil powers, during the time when he was a human.

Long time back . . .

John was sleeping on his bed in his bedroom, (The room was in light blue color, it was a medium size room, with a small balcony attached into it and also a small bathroom which was place at the right side of the bed with the distance of 2mt. there was a golden color cross hanging on the wall, under which there was a desk on which there was an open laptop, a glass of water in which there was a red old rose, and there were also some documents laying on the desk.

At the left side of the bed there was a wooden made closet which was in brown color standing and also close to John's bed there were two small wooden tables, on one of them there was an alarm clock and on the other, there was a frame in which there was a picture of John and Sara. There was a huge hanging lamp on the ceiling of the room too which looked like several attached grapes.)

John was sleeping very deeply, and he was covering himself by a scarlet color blanket, but suddenly he woke up and while panting and sweating, he started looking around the room and then at the clock which was on the table, the clock was showing 7:00am. John got up from his bed, made his bed, started stretching and warming up a little bit, and after a while he went to bathroom and took a shower, he came out of the bathroom and while he was topless, he started drying his hair by his towel, he then spread the navy color curtains and then opened the door of the balcony and went on it, he started looking around and at the people who were walking in the street, he looked at the activities they were doing, as far as he could see was misery, corruption and violence. On each shop, building and cloths there were the pictures of God.SED, in some of the pictures, he was Dancing, singing, kissing, blessing and also cursing, while John was looking at all of these things, a group of homeless young boys and girls entered the street and started breaking the glasses pushing people around and getting violent with the children playing around the area, John noticed one of these boys was raping a woman, the rest of the gang members were laughing, screaming by seeing the view, even the people who were crossing from the place were encouraging them to continue, while the woman was getting raped, one of the gang members broke a glass of the Cursed Blood* (Cursed Blood was the stolen blood of the Twin Cancer Patients from the hospital, the blood would terminate the brains proper activities and would cause of sudden death)

The blood was spread in the face and the mouth of the girl which caused her to die instantly, John couldn't tolerate and felt like he had to throw up, he immediately moved back inside the room, shut the door of the balcony and started breathing deeply as he didn't feel good at all.

After a while John stood beside his bed, pushed the bed a little bit down and then slowly hit the wall behind it, part of the wall slowly opened and a very old wooden and dusty box came out of it, John slowly removed the box and opened it, there was a voice recorder device in the box, John removed the device and while walking around his room he switched it on and began to record his voice.

JOHN (RECORDING)

Hey! beloved people who will get a chance to listen to this recording after you find it, it's me Mr. talking too much, Oh! God damned this mic it doesn't work anymore, Oh! wait a second it works, of course it works, it is my brain which doesn't work anymore, Jesus Christ lalala lololol ah what am I saying?, Let's get serious, as my previous recording was discovered by my lovely Nanny and was flashed in the toilet, I had left by no other choice except recording this new tape again.

Okay! there we go again, my name is John Seven, don't ask why seven, even I don't know myself, I know I was born in Persia, and I was raised by the world around me as I kept traveling from one country to the other at all time but at the present moment I am in Canada where now is called Peace Land, its name has been changed by God.SED, around two years ago we did fight against him but he has magical powers and made most of the people to love him and after creating a peaceful relationship with us he called this place Peace Land, I know my Mum was from Russia and my Dad was from Persia but I never have seen them, never have seen any picture from them, I just know that they were both killed in a very bad car accident which has been unknown to me till the present day, I even don't know who my Grandparents are, I know! poor me!, but I don't really pay attention to it any more as I have the world's number one Nanny who has been like my Mum, Dad, Best Friend, Great Protector and so many other stuff, that's why I call her Angel even though she doesn't like it but I still call her because she really is like an Angel, I forgot this, you may wanna know why on earth am I recording my voice and telling you all of these!?, okay! then listen, around two and a half years ago, as it has been seen and proved too, God has entered the Earth and now he lives among us, his name is SED but don't get crazy I and many people don't believe he is the one yet, as the way he entered the world and the way he does the things haven't been the same from the things we read in the Holy Books so I believe the real God is about to come so I am recording right now so that if the whole world gets terminated or somehow you find this recorder you will know the truth about this fellow who calls himself GOD (while John was recording, Nanny knocked the door, and said: are you awake Johnny?, your breakfast is ready!)

John quickly threw the recorder under his bed and then opened the door,(a short, fat lady was standing at the door, she had white hair, pale eyes and face, large breasts and bottom, wearing a gray color dress and was holding a tray on which there was a glass of water in which there was a new red rose, a plate on which there were two roasted eggs, three pieces of brown bread, on the tray there was also a glass of milk and a bottle of cherry jam.

Nanny (looking at John) said:

Shall I get older than this or you want me to die by standing at this door and then you pull my body inside? John: (smiling) replied, you never need my permission to enter Angel and then he bowed and said: please enter your highness, Nanny entered the room, she then changed the old rose with the new one, she laid the tray on the desk and while going out said: John you better wear something you may catch cold my dear and then left the room. After closing the door John jumped and took his recorder from under his bed and then started recording again.

John (recording):

Sorry guys for the delay there was some situation back in here so I had to cut the conversation, okay what was I saying? Aha! yes, I want to tell you this that I don't trust this God at all, I mean its true he really showed and have done great stuffs that are impossible for any human to do but I still can not believe in him as I believe in the true Living God, in the scripture was written there will come many false prophets who will lead many astray, and the lawlessness will arise up high, many will loose their faith, but the one who keeps his belief and faith till the end will be the winner and will be saved, so I am doing the same thing, well I see this creature is different but (he raised his voice) said: I will wait and fight for the true God not this guy who keeps changing. It`ll be good if I tell you about him a little bit but it would be better if I tell about myself, my unknown family and my Nanny first.(before he spoke, he grabbed a piece of bread, put it in the eggs, ate it and drank some milk after that)

John (recording):

Okay, I am 22 years old, as I have mentioned I know that I was born in Persia but I was raised by the whole world as I kept traveling a lot, I am 182cm tall, having brown hair and eyes, physically fit as I love exercising which is good for health, I am a very religious person, I don't have proper job as I never needed it as my family left me a plenty of money which never ends which is good isn't it? Naa! it is not because it makes you feel lazy, and self satisfied, I keep spending my money as charity, oh boy!, I spend a lot for charity as this is one of the duties which we have. I work as an volunteer at the Twin Cancer Hospital, you may wanna know what is Twin Cancer, well it is not cancer or any disease, it is the curse from the God.SED, see this is how it works like, if any human does anything against God.SED and make him very angry he will then curse that person which means an Evil soul enters inside that person's body, and after that that person will have two different characters, just like two persons in the same body, but frankly speaking the evil soul is the demon itself, yes so many bad things are happening in here which makes me feel crazy as I can't do anything to stop it. I have finished my high school but couldn't go to college as there is no collage left on earth anymore, the reason is that God.SED made it clear that if someone wants to get more knowledge and information more than the level of the schooling system, he or she can simply walk to him and get blessed which everybody is doing at the present moment, so since that day colleges and universities and other high educational institutions were all closed, the problem is, the one who goes to him to get more knowledge comes back more co-co ya its true! The blessed people behave really abnormally, frankly they start thinking about biological contacts more than any other things, sad isn't it?

Okay! enough of me, let me tell you about my unknown parents, hey! did you hear that? (a group of people were screaming and shouting outside on the street) John went on the balcony and started looking at the people who were protesting and continued recording:

Oh! every day is like this, a group of true God believers, just come out, give some slogans and then get beaten, arrested and finally are taken to the Temple and after a while come back co-co, but what a spirit, fighting for the true God, look at them they are from different religions but work totally united as a peaceful Holy family (protestors were shouting God is good all the time, all the time God is good). After few minutes, John said: there they come again P.SED guys, now these people are in danger, (P.SED members attacked the protestors, beat them as bad as they could, arrested them all, killed some of them and then took the rest away) (John while looking very disappointed and upset, went back to his room and closed the door and shut the curtains, he then grabbed another piece of bread, put it in the jam and while chewing drank some milk) and continued recording,

John: these P.SED guys are very dangerous; some of them are very tiny but have the power of a lion well they are all blessed by their God, anyways these guys mostly wear dark gray T-shirts which has two golden color stripes on it, they wear very tight black pants, always have black shades and black shiny shoes, they wear tie too and they have the latest image of God.SED tattooed on their necks, the coolest part about them is that they can really jump high, I mean very high, and they can hear very well, at the moment some of these protestors come out these guys also come by jumping from the buildings and cars or any other places but as today I mostly have seen them coming from inside the sewage lines and man holes ahh! but smell as good as a Rose, it's crazy I know but this is the world I am living in (he smiled), they don't have any sense or any feelings at all, in winter and summer they look the same as well as in fighting, one day one of my good friends accidently hit one of them, the P.SED guy looked like a small kid but she kicked my friend from back and broke his back which caused of his Death(he got tears in his eyes) and then blessed my friend, but he was no longer my friend, he turned into a wild animal, at the moment he opened his eyes he ran towards an old lady and started raping her, (he cleaned his tears) oh man! I am so happy that you guys are not in the world that I am living right now, the worse thing is that no one cries anymore, God.SED doesn't like tears, what type of a God he is (he got angry), if anyone cries will be immediately arrested and then taken away, he made us to loose our feelings, we have become like machines, have no feelings, ahh! anyway let me now talk about my Super Nanny, she is the best, she is everything that a human desires, she has been my best friend since the day I remember, I used to call her Mum but she told me not to as she told me my Mum lives up high and watches me every moment so she may feel sad, but believe me she had been more than anything and anyone in this world to me I love her a lot. Nanny's physical body and face never changed, I know! I know it is not believable but believe me she looks the same as she looked before, but her hair turned white which is the good sign that this lady is normal, She is a very nice and a very calm lady, she helps everyone who she can, and does a lot of charity as well, she usually fears nothing but she is extremely afraid of God.SED, I don't know why? She never goes out when God.SED is around, she specially never goes out of the house when is dark, well I don't really get her but I adore her a lot and owe her a lot.(he then grabbed the last piece of bread put in the rest of the eggs and while eating drank his milk) then started recording:

I almost forgot telling you about my childhood, I had the best childhood that any kid could ever have, I never got sick, never ever, I was the sharpest and the most active student in all the schools and the classes I went, (he then heard footsteps sound as nanny was coming up from the stairs, so he quickly opened his closet wore a light blue T-shirt on which there was a picture of God.SED, and wore his JOJO* (JOJO was the new name of blue pants which looked like Jeans, he then combed his hair and hid the recorder under his bed, meanwhile Nanny entered the room and while singing a song picked the tray and went out, so John got his recorder back and sat on his chair and started recording):

Ya! I was saying that my childhood was very good, I used to make a lot of friends everywhere I used to go and had really good time, I grew up learning about The Holy Son of God, Jesus Christ which has been my highest honor and blessing that I was a little boy but had received the glory and the love by coming to this faith, so I grew up following the rules of religion, did whatever I could to make God proud even I haven't had physical contacts except some kisses (he laughed) with my girl friend as we both believe it would be the act of adultery, and because we haven't had the perfect time to get married, we just have been together for couple of years now,

Okay! enough about the childhood, now let's go to the teenage hood, my teenage hood was involved in many traveling, me and Nanny kept traveling from one country to the other, I travelled to Turkey which is now called Turka, then to Irag which is now called Oil land then I went to India the Spices Land, then I went to France the Water Land and many other places, the cool part is that we never faced any problems, not financially, not socially, not physically which made me adore God for that as I felt extremely blessed by him, I finished my high school two and the half years ago and met Ms. Sara Thomson in those days, oh boy! she is bomb, she is the hottest and the best, she was born in England which is now called Water Land as well and she had the same tragically story like mine, we both work at the same place the Twin Cancer Hospital and the best part is that her money source is too unlimited as her father had written in his Death Note that after he died the money which was left from him would be given to my Nanny to be taken cared of which, has been taken cared. So ya this is what has happened to me in short. Our work is very tough, as the Twin Cancers suffer a lot; we are in charge of making them calm, talk to them and give them hope, play with them if they are young, ahh! (he put his head down) they die very painfully, their pain is unlimited, no medicine cures them as they are cursed, we haven't seen any improvement in any one of them till today, as they die quickly, after getting the curse they survive for three days only and then they expire, many people raised this question that what happens after they die but never got the proper answer back, while speaking he looked at the picture on his T-shirt and said: oh I hate you, you evil creature, you can eat shit and go back to where you came from, If I wouldn't have the responsibility of taking care of my Nanny and hot girl friend I would definitely join the protestors and fight against this Evil creature.

It's better if I talk about him (God.SED) more than myself, meanwhile he switched his laptop on and then on the site called SED The Information*(it was the name of the site, where all the information regarding everything was available), so after awhile of searching, John got angry and said:

nonsense!, whatever written in here is false and untrue, I will tell you the truth, I have seen everything with my own eyes.

Here we go, SED came around three years ago, there came a huge Earth quake, we heard that the source was from Middle East, somewhere near the old Caspian Sea, the whole world was shaking that day, and guess what happened the Waves worked reversal, which recombined the continents and attached them all together same as we had heard in the geography about the history of the continents, millions of people died in that day, buildings collapsed, Oceans flowed on the lands and acted like a washing machine, within few hours, the whole world was destructed. The Sky turned dark, darkness covered the whole world, no one could see anything anymore, and suddenly a very huge lightening stroke the place where was the source of Earth Quake and acted like a huge atomic bomb, it was terrible and very scary, it was supernatural, and unthinkable, and after the explosion the light came back on earth but everywhere was misty and foggy, you may wanna know how did I survive or where I was? I was sitting in my plane, hugging Sara as tight as I could and covering her head with my hands, and Super Nanny was flying the plane, ya I know! she does a lot of things, she drives, rides, flies and unbelievably dances, anyway even though after the lightening and the Earth Quake everything was ruined, the Earth was destructed but Nanny knew exactly where we were going and it was like nothing was happening to us and the plane which made me to adore God more than ever, the strange part is that the same day morning, Nanny was behaving abnormally, she was running this side then that side, me and Sara were sitting on the sofa and were looking at her moves, she told us to sit and get ready as she wanted to take us to Turka which made us pretty excited, so we were in the plane and were witnessing all of the things happening around us. After almost six hours not knowing about where we were going, the mist disappeared, and our eyes popped out, it was like nothing had happened to the Earth, it never looked that beautiful as that day, it was a sunny day, blue sky, clean air, and amazing, Nanny found the direction again and we flew not to Turka but towards the incidental place, and we landed almost crushingly near some unknown place, when we got off the plane our mouths fell down, the place looked like a Postal Cart, that beautiful, thousands of people were standing around and wondering what had happened to Earth, everything looked normal except the land shape which looked very different as continents were attached together again, so many new hills and up and downs were being noticed, Nanny told to me and Sara to follow her and we started getting close to the incidental place, but suddenly she said: move back run!, me and Sara were totally freaked out, we thought she had gone a bit co-co, we ran as much as we could and once again the darkness covered the whole world, everybody was screaming, running towards God knows where and crying out loud, I could see nothing, until saw something which I wish I didn't, six bright falling stars hit each other in the space and a very sharp piece of them which look like a sword came towards the place where we were standing, Sara screamed so loud that I thought I would loose my ears that day, Nanny held my hand even though I couldn't see her and loudly said: John Sara close your eyes, we closed and I felt something it was like the feeling you get when you stand in a moving plane or any vehicle, and then she said: you may now open your eyes, when we did we were almost paralyzed Sara hugged me tight and said: Nanny is an Alien save me John!, you can't imagine within closing and opening of our eyes, we were taken long distance away from the place were the fallen star was falling at, I tried to say what on Earth had happened, but the star stroke the land but there exist no explosion the sword shape piece of star slowly entered the land and went down, just like cutting a piece of butter by a sharp knife, and because it was the only object which was glowing, the whole world could see and be witness of everything, after it went inside the land the whole Earth shook, and from the place where the sword entered there came out a huge, glowing temple, it looked just like the described Temple of King Solomon in the Holy Books, it was the only light full spot on the Earth and after a short time, the darkness disappeared. People were totally freaked out, because just within few minutes ago, almost every single living creature on the planet had died and now they were all alive and standing right beside each other, while everyone was asking and wondering, a massive army made by almost every country of the world reached to the place, boy! I haven't seen such scene even in the movies but anyway we were all scared and also very thank full that we were safe, after awhile several Presidents, Prime Ministers, Kings, Queens and other V.I.P guys came to appearance, one of the Presidents took a Mega Phone and said: welcome to earth you beloved space neighbors!, a lightening came out of the temple and stroke him into several parts, boy you had to see the moment, every single human being attacked the Temple with everything that they could attack with, it was like some fire work was going on in there, the very interesting part about the Temple was that all the bullets, rockets, grenades, sticks, stones which were being thrown and shot into it, were being observed in the temple, it was like people were shooting the stuffs towards a giant sucking hole, these attacks continued for almost three days. As the continents were attached people from different countries got the opportunity to reach themselves to the incidental place, the attachment was good actually as many families members and friends and other people who haven't seen each other for long times got the chance to meet and at the other hand many people were upset because many countries which were enemy with each other were now attached so it was something for itself you know? (John shook his hand), anyways more than normal people, the reporters and the news guys were gathered around the Temple, no one could see inside of it as there was a very huge marble made wall around it and its gold made gates were closed, so everybody were asking questions and the armies were no longer attacking as it was useless and was the wastage of time, so people were just standing and chatting with each other, they have also made several tents around the Temple so they could rest in them and focus on the all the activities which might have happened in the Temple. Those three days were the best days of my life as Sara never stopped holding my hand even for a second, with a small noise she used to jump on me and hid her face behind my back, and I used to sing the LOVE song in my heart (haha he laughed), well the bravest was Nanny she was sitting at the door of our tent and was acting like a watch dog well frankly speaking she looked like a wolf to me (he laughed again), the very strange thing about those days was the Death of billions of true God believers, we heard the Holy places like Churches, Mosques, Temples and other places were all evacuated, just like no believer was left on the Earth which really made me suspicious, and made Nanny very angry.

Anyway, as the things had calmed down at the beginning of the 3rd day, we felt a very weak Earth Quake, it was like something was coming out of the land, for few seconds the vibrations continued and a very strange mist covered the whole area, I remember Sara was hanging on my back and was whispering in my ear this (John you didn't marry me and we are going to die and next life you will forget all about me) (he laughed again) crazy girl friend of mine, okay I was telling you this, after couple of minutes the mist disappeared and all the people`s jaws fell down, there he was Mr. God. SED, he was sitting on soft large golden color chair which was at the top of a very tall and large marble made pillar which had very high altitude, and he was watching everyone from the top of the place, opps! Excuse me!) John had received an email from Sara in which was written that she would be there within an hour) and then John continued: the guy was glowing so much, he had a very large stomach, long black curly hair, he was about 152 or 153cm not more, and was wrapped by a very strange material which looked like the skin of several snakes, suddenly trumpet noise started coming out of the temple, and its two large gates had been opened, behind the door there were thousands of P.SED guys, standing in a very proper lines, and started coming out one by one, they stood all around the wall and secured the area, people were excited and totally out of control too, some wild teenagers had taken of their cloths and were cutting their skins and colleting the blood coming out of them and while shouting were saying: take it all and take us inside!, several people started singing and welcoming the God.SED, the others were just dancing and cheering, people felt it was the end, and all were ready to see what would happen next, middle of the crowd there was a small black boy, standing right beside his parents who were praying to the true God, the kid moved as close as he could to the Temple and shout, he said: Jesus Christ will kick your ass!, boy I just couldn't control myself, everyone started laughing but the laughing turned into crying, God.SED opened his mouth and then closed and the kid fell on the ground and died, we couldn't believe of what we were looking at, I became super angry and suddenly felt something was pumping in my body, I never felt it before, it was like an unlimited source of energy, I felt like I could fly as my body turned very light, when Nanny noticed this, she held my hand very tightly and said: control yourself my dear as the time has not yet come for you, I didn't understand what she said because I could feel nothing except the power inside me, the parents of the kid just fell on the ground and cried out loud, they begged God.SED to forgive their child and give his life back, the rest of the people were scared too and were slowly moving backwards, and then God.SED opened his mouth and closed it again, you can't believe the kid got his life back, the every one who saw it cheered and praised him, thousands of people sacrificed several animals for the sake of him, I was frankly very confused, I didn't know whether I had to believe in him or not, it wasn't the way which was written in the holy books, but the guy had unnatural power which was unexplainable, after awhile, God.SED stood up and with loud voice said: it is good to be back on what I have created, from now onwards my will be done, dwell as much as you can and let me bless you and your children and this generation, people just went crazy, men and women cried for him and many perished too, even Sara started jumping around (slowly he said crazy girl), many reporters started asking different questions from him like, are we going to die? Is it the end of the world? Where is your Holy son? Where are your Holy Prophets? Are you going to judge us for what we have done? How long will you stay? Why did you come anyway? And suddenly God.SED stroke the reporter who asked that and turned her into a piece of Poop, people turned white and black, many perished right away, kids started crying, by seeing these things God.SED controlled his anger and said: my children why are you forsaking me? The world has just begun, what Holy son? What Holy Prophets? Why should I judge you for the deeds you have done? Am I not the God of love? The Creator of Heavens and the Earth? I will live with you forever and ever from now onwards and will never leave you again, when he said the last line, I felt the power in me raised higher, I felt a great heat in my hands, I started seeing better, I started smelling better, I could feel better, but Nanny held my hand again and said: John wait as I have told you! I wanted to ask her what was she talking about but God.SED started speaking again, he said: I have reunited the whole world so there will be no separations, no sorrow, no tears, and I will be able to have you all under my control, while he was speaking I was hearing a different voice coming out of his mouth, it was like a slow motion scene, especially when he said control, he then continued saying: there will be no sickness, no more difficulties in any aspects of your lives, there will be no more injustice, no more violence and crime if you just worship me and let me bless you all, and he raised his hands up, a cloud appeared in the sky and a wind blew into people, people were just drunken by his words and were crying like small babies, he then said: love me and let me love you as I am the God of love, I command you all to worship me as your God and follow my rules as your commander, therefore I shall grant you the things you will desire and several lightening stroke him which made him brighter, people went crazy, I remember an old man who was standing naked and had written on his chest take me my lord! take me and make me young again!, Oh! horny old people (he smiled), the P.SED guys shouted and said: praise the God.SED most high and the sound of trumpets were heard, after awhile of cheering and singing and dancing for his glory, an Asian man stepped forward and said: my lord, may I have the honor of asking you why do your servants call you SED? God.SED looked at him and replied: you may never ever question your God about the things he do! The Asian man put his head down and fell on the ground and said: forgive me my lord for making you disappointed in me, God.SED said: (loudly) I am the owner of your Souls, the maker of my Earth, and the only one who gives you your Directions that is why I am called the God.SED, after hearing this I felt something else in me, in was like something had spread in my body but after a while I started feeling normal again, God.SED continued: my children I will need you all to dwell as much as you can, and let me bless your children, I command you all to surrender your daughters who are virgin to me as their wombs are Holy for me and through them I can get more powers when I heard that I was like come again? The God wants to have virgin girls? Then what about us? And suddenly a question popped in my head, I looked at Sara, she was a virgin too and looked very happy by if she would loose her virginity for that Monster, I almost had a heart attack, I had no idea what to do! Meanwhile God.SED said: my servants will now walk among you and collect your virgins and the P.SED guys started moving towards us, several virgins stood in the lines, some of them even were putting make up on their faces ahh! wild girls(he nodded), and then I looked at Sara again, held her hands and said: Sara who is your only soul mate?, she was looking at the P.SED guy who was coming closer to us, she replied: you sweetie, I said: then you don't need to give your Treasure Island to a pirate as I am its rightful honor right? Sara while waving her hand said: but John, he is God and you never wanna have the treasure anyway!, boy I felt so gayish in that moment, she was right many times we wanted to have good time but I just rejected as I believed and believe of what is written in the scripture, the P.SED guy was coming forward, I looked around and didn't see Nanny around so I just grabbed Sara from her arms and plant a big kiss on her lips, it was the first time that I had kissed her, so many things were going around in my mind I didn't know I was doing it right or wrong either, I was feeling shy too, but I said be the man son show her who`s the rightful owner of the Treasure Island, boy we continued and continued, a P.SED guy came near us and by seeing how passionately we were kissing, he said: praise the lord God.SED for this couple have been blessed, by hearing this everybody started kissing, old, young even kids, so the P.SED guys collected the virgins and took them inside the temple and then gave them to God.SED, me and Sara were yet kissing but everything got blown away, as Nanny squeezed the ear out of me, she said: what are you two doing? While kissing Sara I replied: nothing just practicing, Nanny pulled me back and said: stand properly you wild souls, don't forget you are not yet married and you must not commit adultery, I was not hearing what she was telling me I was just looking into Sara`s eyes, boy blue as sky, but I controlled myself again and replied: of course Nanny, you are correct, Sara pinched me and said: you told me you kissed no one before then how did you know how to do it so well? I was like really!? you liked it? Then I thought how did she know how to do it so well? And I asked the same question, she said that she practiced in front of mirror and on many pillows, when Nanny heard us both she was like active volcano, she said: what have you done to your souls, couldn't you wait until you would get married and be attached with each other by your souls, where have your faith gone? Me and Sara while putting our heads down slowly replied: sorry Nanny it won't happen again, and then we started paying attention to the things which were happening at the Temple, the virgins were standing beside God.SED and were waving to people, God. SED said: (loudly) remove your cloths my children, we were like what? Naked virgin girls from different colors and races! Men and women turned horny, even handicaps looked very excited too, but I miss the view as my possessive girl friend closed my eyes and when she opened them, the virgin girls were wrapped by red robes, God.SED looked at the people and said: for I am the Alpha and The Omega, and he then touched the virgins bellies, and within a blink of eyes they all turned pregnant, I guess nine months sharp, innocent girls were shocked and also couldn't bare the pain and the weight they just got, and then God.SED said: and I am the father of all nations, the virgins started giving birth, people were like crazy, the impossible was done possible right in front of our eyes, who could have done such supernatural activity, several P.SED guys jumped on the pillar and collected the new born babies and took them inside the Temple, and amazingly the virgins stood up, just like nothing had happened to any one of them, by seeing this I even got amazed, the whole world cheered and worshiped him, oppss! I am sorry I gotta go to bathroom (after few minutes) excuse me for that, so then while God.SED was kissing the virgins foreheads said:, I command you all to dwell at all times, and let me be in full control, another great wind was blown from the Temple towards everyone and suddenly a mist covered around God.SED, no one could see him anymore, after few seconds the mist disappeared and people`s jaws fell down again as God.SED physical appearance and cloths were changed and improved, he had got brown hair, he looked 165cm may be less than that, he was wrapped by robes which looked like the skin of the leopard and he looked very stronger as well he then said: I have received your love and I will bless you all forever. As far as I could see, people were rejoicing, cheering, and extremely have gotten involved into physical activities which was embarrassing to look at, Nanny took a deep breath and said: as I was told, I looked at her and asked: what? She nodded and replied: let`s go home,

Sara was still pinching me and biting my ear, after awhile we got into the plane, when we sat on our chairs Sara jumped on my legs and said: you have been a bad boy Mr. Seven and started smiling, when Nanny saw it, she rushed to us and said: have you forgotten you are not yet married? Where is your faith? Behave children behave, for you do not know of what you are doing! Sara replied with a very round British accent: we have not forgotten anything at all Nanny don't worry so much, Nanny while making faces went to the cockpit and prepared to fly, Sara held my hand, put her head on my chest, and said: we need to get marry soon, boy my heart started beating faster (he laughed), I said: ya of course we must do it faster, then Sara looked at me and said so??? I didn't know what to say? I replied: soon! soon! no objections your highness! and we went back to Peace Land.

Ding Dong, Ding Dong (the door bell was ranged) (Sara had arrived and was pressing the bell button again and again) John immediately switched his recorder off and hid it inside the box and then put the box where it was, took the SED50 (the money in the shape of note which is equal to $5000 from his desk case and rushed downstairs to welcome Sara, meanwhile Nanny had opened the door and was hugging Sara, by seeing them John too hugged them both, Sara tried to kiss Johns lips but John kissed her forehead instead which made her very angry, and then John asked whether she wanted to have something to eat or drink, and Sara angrily replied :yes you better get me something with sugar in it, Nanny while smiling said: I know what exactly you guys need and then moved towards the kitchen, John kissed Sara`s hand and said: forgive me your majesty but we need to get married which we will soon, and then I will steal your treasure and secure the area with many soldiers, Sara laughed and said: go wash your mouth with soup, naughty boy and while laughing they entered into the kitchen, (the kitchen was made by wood and was large and was in brown color, it was an open kitchen which was attached to the main dining room, there was a long table standing at the middle of it, around which there were eight wood made chairs all in dark brown color, at the top of the table on ceiling, several pans and kitchen stuff were hanging, and also there were many wooden cabinets all around the wall, from the entrance point of the kitchen to the left, there were a large wine red fridge and freezer on which they were so many pictures of John, Nanny and Sara, the floor was parquet which was in semi dark brown, and from the entrance point to the north side there were two large windows under which there were two sinks and couple of clean plates which were around it, the kitchen was covered by flowers mostly red roses, it was as clean as crystal, everything that a kitchen needed was available in there)

While talking John and Sara sat on the chairs, Nanny took couple of homemade cookies out of the oven and while she was pouring pine apple juice in the glasses she laid them all in front of Sara and John and said: enjoy! So Sara and John kept talking and eating, and after awhile, Sara looked at her hand watch and said: John we are late Harry up! we gotta go fast, today some new T.C patients will arrive and we will need to take care of them, so after saying bye to Nanny they went out of the house, but before they go, Nanny hugged them and said: your parents would be proud of you two, and then they left the house.

While walking in the street, John stopped and said: Hallelujah girl you look like a blasting bomb today, actually Sara was wearing a light pink T-shirt on which there was a picture of God.SED and was wearing a tight dark pink pant, and red sport shoes, and also the cross that John had given for her, Sara looked at John and said: do you like it, you`ll need to see what I am wearing under these and pinched John`s arm, John looked at her in a funny way and said: well I will see it after you are called Mrs. Sara Seven, while they were talking a group of protestors entered the street so John and Sara moved from the street and then stood near a fruit shop, Sara started laughing, John looked at her and asked: what is the matter sugarcane ? Sara pointed towards the protestors and said: its too funny that Christians, Muslims, Jews and the rest are standing beside each other and giving slogans against God.SED, John smiled and said: it is actually very beautiful, what would have happened if the world looked like this from the beginning, after all these years they have now come to know about the truth of this world but its too late I hope their faith will make the true God to have mercy on us and come to save creation, Sara interrupted saying John do you still believe that there is another god, even after seeing the things that God.SED has done? John immediately looked at her and said: what do you mean Sara? Then he picked a grape and said: look at this Sara, look at its design, from such a brown hard roots and branches such colorful fruit has come out, who could have really done this? SED who claims he is the one couldn't make this fruit this beautiful as he is nothing but a horny creature, he used the history of what happened to Mary mother to black mail people emotionally which he has been successful in it, he (Suddenly a group of P.SED members, while jumping on the buildings, and elsewhere arrived entered the street and beat everyone that they could, while beating the protestors, a small girl fell down, and because people were stepping on her, she losed her life, the P.SED members arrested everyone and took them away, but the dead body of the small girl was still there) John looked at Sara and said: do you know what I mean now Sara? Then he put his hands on Sara`s shoulders and said: do you still believe in the one who has created us Sara? But before Sara replied a group of Virgin collectors and Love makers* (Virgin collectors were former prostitutes male and female who were in charge of collecting virgin men and women and take them to the temple, even though the temple was very far from there but it was their duty to do so, they had no proper cloths, their chests, breasts and bottoms were covered by black piece of leather and they had black leather sandals, they had two large diamonds on each side of their shoulders which was their identity prove and the latest picture of the face of the God.SED which was always changing) and Love makers*(love makers were former pimps, men and women were in charge of seeing who was involved in any physical activities and who wasn't, they were wearing light purple robes on which there were two red stripes, and had golden color sandals, if they would find anyone who wasn't involved in any physical activities, they world arrest that person and in front of everyone start having physical activity with him or her which would cause in the end of the life of that person, so everyone were very much afraid of them and would do anything to make their taste satisfied) entered the street from north side of it, at the moment people saw them, left their works and whatever they were doing and got involved in physical activities, John noticed a man kissing the lips of his own dog and was petting her passionately, when Sara saw them, she just jumped on John and started kissing him wildly as she found an excuse and a great opportunity, while John was kissing her he slowly opened his eyes and kept looking at the groups and the people around them, he noticed that some young girls were screaming at their parents to help them and stop them from being taken but their parents were too busy kissing and doing some other things that almost made them deaf of hearing their daughters voices, many young people also were getting raped by the love makers, by seeing this John felt the same power which he felt years ago and started getting warmer, while Sara was kissing him said: oh you like it don't you baby, can`t wait to get you on the bed, after few minutes, the groups left the street, what was left was nothing but misery, many parents had losed their children, many people couldn't believe of what they had done, it was like everyone had been hypnotized during the arrival of the groups. Even though Sara wasn't getting separated from John, he stopped kissing her and said: Sara control yourself, they are gone, Sara opened her eyes and angrily, crossed her arms and stood beside him, John held her hand and said: Sara do you still believe in the true God? Sara angrily replied: yes! yes! are you happy now? John kissed her hand and said: I feel something big is going to happen which will put the world in jeopardy and then while holding Sara`s hand they walked to the Twin Cancer Hospital.

The whole world was changed, the way of wearing cloths, the life styles, the way of cultures, traditions, behaviors, designs, the constructions, every things and every way of living was changed. The buildings were being made in the shape of fruits, wonders, people`s faces, and in other exotic shapes. The vehicles shapes were changed too, most of them had seven tires and the rest had more than that, planes were removed from the face of the world as God.SED had involved his own authorities in the air so that he could have an eye above everything from the top, Most of the people used to travel by the new super fast train which would cross from one country to the other within a very short time. Even the weather changing cycle and timing was changed, as God.SED has taken over its control and according to his taste he would change the weather but he would have announced it before he would change it so people could prepare themselves and also get warned.

The hospital that Sara and John were going to, was a triangular shaped building which was very huge and tall, it had several floors, very well made and constructed, included number one helping and healing facilities, and was amazingly clean and well maintained, the color of the building was light orange, and it had three blue stripes as well.

After reaching to the Hospital, John as usual opened the door and while bowing said: please enter Madam, Sara while keeping her noise up replied: thank you dear and then they both entered the hospital.

The color of the floor was light blue, and the walls were in green color. Every floor looked extremely clean and shiny. There were several nurses and doctors moving from one place to the other. The nurses were wearing long cream color dresses and had a large orange hat on their heads from which they would take their items out and put them back, even though the hat looked small but it had enough space for each and every items. The nurses had large diamond rings on their hands too which were given to them as gifts by God.SED, but in fact, the rings were the price which was paid to them after having biological contacts with God.SED, and the doctors who were moving around and pretending that they were doing something, were wearing gray robes, and had two shining Jasper on their shoulders.

As usual John and Sara started going from one room to the other and started checking the updates and writing their reports.

After getting some patients reports, John went to another room to see a patient`s condition, but at the moment he opened the door he stood stunned, the nurse inside the room was kissing the patient who was just a little boy. John couldn't believe it, he immediately rushed towards the nurse, grabbed her and pushed her backwards which made her to fall down, and then took a look at the small boy as he was really worried of his well being, but there was something strange with that boy, he looked like a mature man, so by seeing this John shouted out loud and called Sara who was working at the next room. Sara rushed to him and by seeing the abnormal activities happening in the room, she immediately ran to call a doctor, meanwhile John was holding the small boy in his hand and was looking at the nurse cautiously, as it was the first time that a nurse had also got the T.C, John had no idea that what she could do and what she was planning to do next. The nurses eyes were stretched back, and her teeth seemed longer than the normal size, she looked very darken as well and her eye balls were rolled back and had appearance of a cat, even the small boy looked the same but he had long beard as well which had never been seen by anyone until that day.

After few seconds, the boy and the nurse started shaking abnormally, the small boy stood with a very unusual speed and started moving towards the nurse, John tried to stop him but the boy pushed John back with an extra ordinary power, therefore John was thrown into the painting at the wall and fell down behind the sofa which was there, the kid moved closer and closer, the nurse opened her legs widely and said: come master come dwell with me as I need you and she started licking her lips, the small boy replied with an evil voice: soon the whole world will be mine, meanwhile John got himself together, and very weakly stood up, by seeing the view he felt the power inside of himself which he felt before, without any specific reason he shouted out loud and said: by name of Father, Son and the Holy Spirit I command you Evil spirits to leave these innocent souls and go back to the place where you have come from and never return, suddenly the boy and girls head turned towards him, John almost had a heart attack as he was very afraid, but then the nurse and the boy looked down and started shaking very badly and started being thrown from one side to the other, and then a dark mist came out of their mouths and went down towards the floor and disappeared. The nurse and the small boy fell on the floor, so John rushed to them, he picked the boy up and put him back on the bed, and before he reached to the nurse, the nurse opened her eyes and very quickly stood up and started cleaning her dress, John then went and stood near her and said: how are you doing now? The nurse was upset, she fell on the floor and grabbed John's pant and replied: I don't wanna go to hell sir please help me, please pray that God forgive me and save me from Evil powers, John's heart pumped faster, he was extremely excited and happy so he raised his hands up and while his eyes were closed, he started praying and adoring God, meanwhile Sara reached with two other nurses and a doctor, while she was chanting, she shout and said: what the heck are you doing with my boy friend in here? The doctor clapped and said: praise the God.SED most high as he makes everyone fall in love, Sara went to John, pushed him back stood between him and the nurse and while pointing her finger at the nurse said: how dare you touching my boy friend`s treasure? John while being very embarrassed, whispered inside Sara`s ear and said: take it easy it's not what it looks like, the nurse turned red and while her head was down, said: thank you for saving me sir, and went out of the room, along with her the doctor and the other nurses too went out.

Sara looked at John and said: what happened to your faith Holy John? You think of marriage when we are all alone but when you are alone with some bitch like that you forget about everything huh? While she was blaming John, the small boy came down from the bed and pulled Sara`s hand and said: uncle John saved my life and the nurse, we had bad things inside us and he healed us, John picked him up and said: I have done nothing it was God who did and then he blinked, Sara was embarrassed and upset, she realized that she acted childishly as nothing had happened between John and the nurse and the amazing part was that the small boy was cured which itself was a miracle, so she felt really disappointed in herself, John then put the small boy down, and wrote on his report documents that he had no problems and was fine and it was a misunderstanding that they had brought this boy in this hospital, and then went near Sara and slowly said: this is the reason we haven't gotten married yet, you still don't trust me and don't let me trust you, Sara couldn't control herself she hugged him while controlling her tears from falling said: I am sorry dear!, I am sorry! I just love you so much!, when I came in and . . . John interrupted by saying: I love you too Sara, whatever happened had happened, forget it sweet heart, it's better that we take the rest of the day off as I don't feel very good, Sara got herself together said: I will talk to the doctor about it now, and she went out, John then went to the small boy and said: remember kid, the one who is protecting us will soon send his massive army to save all of us I am sure, so pray and ask him to protect you and your family members okay? And the kid nodded his head, after awhile Sara came back and together they went back home.

After they reached to home, they removed their shoes off, washed their hands, sat on the chairs in the kitchen and while talking with Nanny they started biting the green apples which Nanny had given them to eat, Nanny brought some cookies and put them in front of Sara and John and sat close to them and asked them how was their day? Why did they come back early? And could they find any way to heal any patients? Sara looked at Nanny and said: well, I haven't found anything but John definitely found something today and did something today, John was in deep thinking and didn't pay enough attention to what Sara had said: so Sara pushed him a little and said hello! Mr. Seven are you in here? John looked around and got himself together and replied: yes of course, I just sort of prayed for a patient and his nurse and they both amazingly were healed, Sara looked at him and said: but you said the kid was totally fine, John tell the truth, no one could ever heal any T.C patient before so what really happened? Nanny immediately interrupted by saying, ah! Its all good, no problems, maybe John has been mistaking, John tried to say something but Nanny continued saying, you both look very tired, so you both better have some hot water bath and rest, but Sara said she had to go and take a look at her house, even though she used to live at Johns house at all time but she often used to go and see her house as she believed her father`s smell was still there. After kissing Nanny and hugging John, she said I`ll go and come back soon before the Night Watchers* come (Night Watchers were group of God.SED new security units who were in charge of moving in streets and look for anyone who was alone, so they would attack and catch the person, scare him or her till Death and then take that person along with them to the place where they came from which was always unknown for people as the Watchers moved with extra ordinary speed. They had no eyes to see but had a very sharp and powerful smelling power, they could feel and smell the fear, so in night they could easily find people who were scared or depressed, and would catch them all, they used to wear black tight leather cloths, from the tips of their fingers to their toes were all covered, they were all bald as well and when they would find some person who was afraid they would turn reddish and make unusual sounds, so before it was too late people used to rush to their homes because no one wanted to get in the hands of these units.)

John looked at Sara and said; you better forget about going out, I don't wanna see my future wife being taken by those monsters, and he then huged her and kissed her on her chick, Sara looked at him and said: since when have you become so worried about your tough future wife huh? Don't worry I will go to Michelle*(Michelle was a Gay boy, he met Sara and John at the high school as they were classmates so since then they were all good friends but John had never trusted him, he felt there was something odd with that boy) first and after there I may go to home, John said: even though I don't like that soft boy but I prefer him more than the house, so when you reach to him call me and don't forget sharing the truth with him, let his heart be touched by the Holy Spirit so his soul might get saved by the lord`s glory, Sara while wearing her shoes replied: how many times do you remind me this, I know future husband what I'll need to do, and then she said bye and went out of the house, at the moment she closed the door Nanny stood beside John and said: did anyone except you see what happened in there? John amazed and wondering replied: no one! but how . . . how do you know about what happened today at the hospital?

Nanny closed the curtains quickly and told to John to go and fresh up, John while being very freaked out, went upstairs to his room to get fresh up, he took a warm shower, wore his home cloths, combed his hair and then while singing a song went downstairs, and then entered the kitchen.

By looking at Nanny, he noticed and realized something wasn't right as Nanny looked very worried and upset, Nanny was sitting at a chair and was biting her lips, when she saw John, she got herself together and said: come my dear boy! Come sit along with me!, she used to speak like that when she wanted to advice John or tell him some news, so John (doubtfully) sat beside her on another chair, but before he spoke, Nanny said: John have you done such thing before? John immediately had a flash back, he remembered the time he was playing with his friend with a ball,back in Turkey and while he was crossing from a street, for the first time he saw Sara who was screaming for help and was being chased by an abnormal man, he remembered that he threw the ball and hit the man right at his head and shout: stop it you jerk or I will break your neck, he remembered when the man turned his face around, his friend (Abdullah) who was standing right beside him peed in his pants and fainted, as the man had no eyes and his appearance was like a wild cat, and had Evil appearance, John thought he was nothing but a demon so he just raised his voice up and said: by the power of my lord Jesus Christ I command you to go to Hell and leave us alone, he remembered the man screamed harshly and hit himself to the wall beside him and broke the wall and entered in the building which was beside him, John remembered he rushed to Sara who had fainted and looked around to see where the man was but he didn't see anything except the people who were looking at him very scared from inside the building, he remembered a man sitting on his chair and the tea inside his tea cup was spreading all over the floor.

After thinking a bit, John looked at Nanny and said: yes!, Nanny smiled and said: why haven't you told me that, if you would have told me I would be able to do a lot in those days to make a safer future for you but now I don't have the power I used to have and moreover I have been informed by the leader that I have to go back home as you have reached to your powers and now are capable to even used them, she then put her head down and said: I can't believe this is happening, I thought I would be the one who would teach you how to use your powers!, John was totally freaked out, he wasn't understanding anything, he put his hands on her shoulder and said: what are you talking about Angel? Who have contacted you? What powers? Nanny smiled and said: from the beginning you were special, you were born by a sparkling Holy layer around your body, every one inside the room was stunned as you were glowing so much, doctor and the nurses tried their best to removed the layer from your face and your body but they couldn't, no scissor, no surgery knife could cut the layer, but your mother removed it with her bare fingers, and then kissed you so many times. John looked upset, angry, and very confused, and asked: what are you talking about Angel? Are you drunk?

Nanny looked at John while having tears in her eyes and said: I tried to help her John, I did, I even tried to help them both but I could do nothing as I haven't had the authorities and her tears started falling down, John put his hands on her shoulder and said: oh! Come one now! Angel take it easy, don't cry, remember we cry we get arrested, Nanny raised her voice and said: I don't care anymore, I hate these sons of bitches, ah Its good to be able to say bad words in this place, she then held Johns hands and said: John I will not be able to protect you anymore, if I stay I will die like a normal human, I wanna go back home and become the one I used to be, do you understand me Johnny? I wanna go see your mum again, I miss her very much, I miss my home my people, your future people. Johns eyes were popped out, he held Nanny's arms and shook her a bit and said: have you started using drugs or have watched some emotional movie again?

She looked into Johns eyes and started shaking abnormally, and a very powerful energy wave was blown from her which threw John into the cabinets and dislocated the stuff which were hanging and standing around the place, after awhile John got himself together and while saying this is the second fly today, he stood up and was amazed, a young lady was standing at the top of the table, she had straight blond and brown hair, her breast and bottom were covered by white feathers just like she was wearing cloths made from feathers, she had two bird looking wings and was glowing so much.

John while being very amazed and shocked said: I knew you were an angel! Nanny looked at John and said: of course I am, and my name is Luzie and I am at your service little Johnny. John's mouth was wide open and its water was dropping down, he controlled himself and said: boy! You look very young, younger than me, it's just like movies, she replied: indeed it is Johnny, then she sat on a chair and said: come sit, I have a lot to talk about. John sat beside her and her beauty drunken John, he was just looking at her body when Luzie said: slowly never look at a woman with lust eyes as the lord have told us, the words just blew a bullet in Johns mind, he turned red and said: amm! you look good, I mean hot but you know you are not my type, I have a soul mate already so no problems, she then said: I know everything about you John but we must follow the heavenly laws at all time so control yourself.

Then John said: wow! All these years you were living with me and protecting me, feeding me, oh! but you have seen me naked too, luzie smiled and said: yes I did. Then John continued saying: why have you done all of these? Luzie replied: I was your mothers best friend just like her sister, we came down to Earth, to research, serve and to stop the humans from sinning. We transformed into human shape and started moving from one country to the other, healing people, helping them in their life aspects, sharing the good news and saving their souls, the most important part was that we were highly forbidden to have feelings for any human or fall in love as we have the pure Holy blood and our connection with a human would cause serious problems and would cause serious circumstances as well, but your mother had the behavior as Sara had now, she couldn't control herself at all and kept looking at this guy and that guy, and finally found your Father in England, he was a missionary from Persia and was in the mission to save the losed souls when he was in London. Your father was a real hotty I must say, frankly speaking he looked just like you but bolder, he looked fit and fine, very handsome, and extremely powerful and faithful in what he was doing, he was a famous man among the church people, through him many souls were saved, he was simply amazing, your mother could smell and feel him even before they met, it was her who found your Dad, we were just crossing from the church were he was preaching at and your mother stood right in front of the doors and said: I found him, we went in and sat on one of the benches, it was funny as when your father looked at your mother he messed up a little bit, he forgot the lines, he had to speak that day, but very quickly got himself together and continued preaching, John interrupted saying Just like movies, then he made his voice softer and said: beautiful! love at the first sight and laughed, luzie laughed too and continued speaking, their love was very pure, very powerful, they were in the skies in those days, I tried to control them but frankly speaking I haven't seen an angel in love with a male human being so even for me it was really fun to experience everything while being with them, they kept romancing. Writing love letters and doing things which resulted you, John laughed, and while listening poured orange juice in two glasses and put them on the table, then while listening slowly started drinking the juice, Luzie too started drinking and continued speaking: I miss heaven, in there we used to go to the orange tree, our friend and used to dance around it, sing a song and the tree used to drop its oranges down for us, but you will not find this type of oranges in here as the oranges in heaven are the purest, they have grown up Holy, not with the help of machines and chemicals, even they taste better than these oranges, John excited said: oh man! I cant wait to see there, then Luzie continued: and then after while your Mum had you in her stomach which was against the rules, and was done without permission, her wild action made the Angels in heaven very angry, as many Angels demanded to live with a human before but they never rejected the laws of Holiness, anyway the time for your birth had come, she was in a lot of pain, as you were and are half human and half angel, John interrupted saying cool!, she then continued: our leader Gabriel came down from Heaven and appeared right beside us in the emergency room, the time was paused, only me, your Mum and father were moving the rest of the world wasn't, leader was very angry, he looked at your mother and said: you have two options heavenly sister, you may give birth to the child on Earth and die because of its pain just like a normal human being and normal soul which will make you forbidden to enter the heaven anymore as you have sinned or come along with me, but your mother loved your father very much, she wanted him to see you, so she decided not to go with The leader, Gabriel didn't really seemed, amazed just like he knew of the decision that your mother was about to take, so he just raised his right hand up and then touched you, and blessed you with the Holy Spirit, after the Holy Spirit entered your body, he looked at me and said: he is the Seventh of the chosen ones, take care of him until he is ready and then disappeared, John was very amazed by the words he was hearing, he realized the reason behind the powerful energy that he felt at different situations, luzie then touched Johns chest and closed her eyes, John felt the energy which he felt before but this time it was like he could feel it moving around his body and suddenly his chest started glowing, Luzie opened her eyes and said: now you can see your invisible Holy Sign, John removed his T-shirt, there was a shining number seventh on Johns right chest, which was in Greek language, John couldn't believe of what he was looking at, he could feel an extreme power rushing through his body from up to down, Luzie touched the sign and said: this is the highest blessing that any creature could ever have. By this sign you have received the power of controlling the Seven Holy Arrows of Light with the power you have received you can now do the impossible possible Johnny. She then said: it was around 3am when The leader left, and the time turned into normal, your mother was in extreme pain, she was crying out loud and shouting, your father was crying too because he knew in a very short time he would be witness of your mother's death, I was crying too for the first time in my human life, when the time had come and you were born, your mother held your fathers hand and said: I love you and then looked at me and in our Angelical language said: take care of my son and then closed her eyes, her soul was taken immediately by the Death

Angel the Death took her down, Johns tears fell down, Luzie continued but she is at Heaven now, John cleaned his face and said what!? Luzie looked at him and replied: while the nurses took you to do the cleaning and the rest took your mother to another emergency room, to try to save her, your father pulled me back in another room and fell on his knees, while crying he started begging me, he said: help me to save my wife`s soul, let me go to Hell but let her soul be saved, I was crying so much at that time I didn't know what to say, and the thing which wasn't supposed to happen, happened The Death Angel came back and made a deal with your father, he said he could take the sins out of your mother and then put them on your father, so your mothers soul would be saved but your father would go to Hell directly after he would die, John said: what you mean directly? Luzie said: after a human dies, his or her soul goes to the place where we call Nowhere Land, which is divided into two parts, a place where looks like Heaven and the other which looks like Hell, John was just quite and listening, then Luzie said: because your father loved your mother most high, he accepted the deal, I could do nothing because the authority and power of the Death Angel is beyond imaginations, so your mothers soul was saved but your father was left with a lot of sins in him, he fell on the floor, because he felt so much pain in his body as the sin committed by an Angel is very high and it is unbearable for any human to survive with such source of sin, I could see his soul screaming for help but I could do nothing, I just prayed for him and cried, I could hear you too, you were crying out loud and wanting milk to drink, I could understand your language as we Angels understand all the languages, this is one of the gift we have, I couldn't bear you crying so after helping Peter. John interrupted my father's name is Peter? Luzie nodded and said: yes his name is Peter, after I helped him to stand up I rushed to the room where you where, it was a rainy night, it looked like the world was crying, I held you in my hands, and kept blessing you by my Holy powers, I was hearing nurses saying that your mother had left the world, so many things were happening at on time, I was just crying, and blessing you, I heard your father's footsteps, he was moving towards the room, but before he reaches, he fell down, I could hear everything, it was like there was no other sound and noise in the building except your fathers movements, I held you tight, and took you to him to let him see you, but I saw Death Angel standing right at the middle of the floor, by the way the time was paused again you know we have special powers, John didn't move at all, the Death smiled and said: welcome to this miserable place my sweet heart, protect the child as he will lead untouchable armies very soon and he disappeared.

I was left alone, with you, your mother's dead body, and your father's dead body; I couldn't tolerate the pain I was feeling so I ran away from there and kept traveling around the World to find the safest place for you to live but wherever we went we had problems which you have no idea about them, John drank some more Orange juice and said: but you told me I was born in Persia, you lied to me huh? Luzie nodded and replied: count that as my sin, it has been because of these small sins that I couldn't go back to Heaven and stood by your side for all these years, John smiled and said: you sacrificed yourself for me huh? That's cool girl, John then got serious and said: do you know what is happening with my father now? Luzie nodded and said: I haven't been there, no one could ever reach till there except the dark powers, John looked very confused and didn't know what to say or even what to ask, he looked at Luzie and said: what power do I have right now? Luzie smiled and said: the promised powers, the Holy Spirit, you haven't been able to use it, because the time wasn't right but now you can use it but be careful, John said: but how can I use it, do I have to say any words like what we see in movies, Luzie laughed and said: why do you keep saying that? This is real John! The abnormal man, the unusual nurse, the small boy, they were all possessed by Demons and you terminated them by the power you have in your body and soul, John (looking very amazed) said: that is just awesome isn't it, can I walk on the water too? Luzie laughed and said: you are crazy Johnny.

After drinking some more juice, John said: oh man! I have bunch of questions that I must ask you!, Luzie nodded and said: I have limited time John, please go ahead and ask me, so John asked her (who is God.SED really?)

Luzie shook her wings and said: he is not one but he is the combinations of the sons of the Satan!, John shockingly said what!?, Luzie replied: SED means Satan, Evil and the Devil, the hair on Johns body stood up as he was very afraid, luzie said: do you remember of what is written in the scripture, the Dragon will be protected by two beasts, John started feeling very scared, and said: yes (very weakly), Luzie said: the Dragon is Satan, or the Lucifer, and the other two beasts are his unholy sons, the unholy Evil and the Devil. John rubbed his eyes a little bit and scratched his head, and said: ahh man! Then the real war which is written in the book is about to come, isn't it? Luzie took a deep breath and replied: yes John; very soon whatever that had been written in the Holy books will come to existence, the P.SED army, the virgin collectors, the Love makers, they are all the Demons which have changed their appearance, in fact they haven't change anything, it's the humans who cannot see them as they have not the power of the truth yet but you my boy you have it in you as you had always so don't be scared if you walk on the street next time as it will be like a very wild Halloween for you, John swallowed the water inside his mouth and said: thank God I am old enough to handle some scary things, and they both laughed a bit. Meanwhile John stood up and poured the glasses with grape juice, luzie picked up the glass and said: ah! I miss home, so much fun we used to have, she was going to tell a story but John interrupted saying, please Angel I mean Luzie we don't have much time as you have told me but hey why don't you have time? Are you going somewhere? Luzie smiled and said: yes I am, I am going back home forever Johnny, don't be afraid!, I will be watching you from the above until the time of plagues, John looked at her very suspiciously and said plagues? Luzie nodded and said: yes the destruction plagues, you have read about them in the Holy Book didn't you? John just nodded his head and replied: yaa! But when will it happen? Luzie shook her wings and said: it may happen soon but as it is written in the scripture, he will come with his army like a thief, collect the souls who have the Holy Sign as you have, and then after all these years, we will fight against Evil armies and this time will terminate them completely, the Judgment Day which is about to come will not be an easy one, every single creature will be judged, young, old, black, white, nothing will be left un judged, even the holiest and the un holiest, the time that has been given to humans, has been perfect and enough, so if the Judgment Day happens no one will have anything to say against Father, John nodded.

John then drank some grape juice and said: wow man! I have to marry Sara as fast as I can, I want to be her husband on Earth and in Heaven, and have her . . . Luzie interrupted saying, it will not happen, John looked at her very suspiciously and asked: what will not happen? Luzie replied: you will not marry Sara as she will not join us in Heaven. John became angry and said why? What is wrong with her? Luzie said: she doesn't believe in the God we believe in, she pretends but she has losed her faith after seeing the unthinkable things that the God.SED has done, John couldn't breathe anymore, he felt the power in him was about to be released, he raised his voice and said: this is not true! She believes in Father, we used to go to church together at all time, we prayed together at all time how is it possible? Luzie looked at him and said: calm down, not everyone who goes to churches, and other worshiping places is the true worshiper and true warrior of Father, John said: but I love her, I will do anything to save her, I will go to Hell if I have to go but will never allow her to be harmed, Luzie smiled and said: the reason of my staying with you all these years wasn't just small sins, it was the love and respect that you have for people which makes you so much like your father, the things which must happen will happen and you may not have any power to stop them but as we know impossible is possible for our maker, but John you can`t imagine of the things which will happen to Earth so take your steps very carefully from now onwards, a small mistake may cause of very terrible consequences.

She continued saying: when I was created, there was a huge battle in Heaven, the battle between Light and Darkness. In that time Lucifer was in charge of leading the Angels but he himself turned his back upon us, many Angels did the same, which made Father very angry and disappointed in creating us, there was nothing but worries in Heaven, every day some explosions were happening, John said: you mean explosions like what happens in war on Earth? Luzie smiled and said: our explosions are different, we have Light Bombs, Light Bombs are energy bombs not like chemical ones they are made from our Holy Spirit, but believe me you don't wanna see or use anyone of them as they may bring some serious destructions, especially if they are blown on Earth. Anyways, many Angels had fallen and many losed their faith, we were almost going to lose the battle but father himself entered in the battle, nothing could stop him, he fought against the Darkness, won the battle like a victorious king and then locked him for thousands of years human years!, John while chewing his nails said wow! Please don't stop keep going on, so Luzie continued: we had failed Father in the battle which we were ready at, we thought we were trained enough to stop the Darkness but I guess we were not,(she took a deep breath), our failure was Fathers failure, we were all upset. But Father never let us feel as we have been defeated as he is the God of love not hate, but after the war father faced his biggest failure which made him furious, John while standing and rubbing his legs on each other said: I gotta go to bathroom it's an emergency, he ran and after awhile came back and said: what was fathers biggest failure, Luzie nodded her head and said: Lucifer, John said: oh ya! I know, but Luzie nodded her head again and said: you know nothing, after the war was ended everything went back to normal, we were all happy again, and we were all reconstructing the kingdom, I was a healer of green plants, I used to go everywhere and design the land by planting different flowers on each side of it, John interrupted saying that's why you kept bringing a Red Rose into my room and you covered this place(he pointed to the flower pots that were standing around the kitchen) Luzie smiled and said: yes you are correct, and continued: no one knows what really made Lucifer to go to the forbidden kingdom which now is called Hell, but he might have felt doing it so, as we Angels have all the feelings that the humans have, John just blinked, Luzie said: when he came back he was different, it was like he was brain washed or something, but because he was the most powerful Angel in those times no one dared to ask any question from him regarding what he used to do, he was the most talented Angel, he was faster than all, he was adored by Father, the playing music was his speciality, he was simply the best, but the idea of the creation of the Earth and the humans made him very angry as he felt our failure made Father to do this, and perhaps it was also the reason that made him to go to the forbidden kingdom as well, John was just quite and listening, she then said: after sometimes Father made the Universe, the Sun, the Moon, the Stars, the Planets, and the Earth which was his best creation until that time, he couldn't stop laughing and rejoicing, we were also very happy, we were dancing at all times, singing and almost had forgotten about our failure. Anyway the time of the creation of Adam & Eve had come, he made them with such accuracy that wasn't seen until that day, he really loved Adam and Eve which made us too proud of having them. Then one day which is called the Sabbath, he rested and he called all of us, he first showed us the work that he had done even though we had seen most of it but it was still very beautiful to see them again and while standing behind the Adam & Eve Father said: these are the best of my creations, you may bow down to them as there are the purest than all, we were very excited because we had to teach them a lot of things and take care of them, the interesting part was that Adam was created in Fathers image but he was totally powerless so it was interesting for us to see some creature who looked like Father but had no blessed powers, so we Angels have all bowed down, even Gabriel bowed down but Lucifer didn't, he even shout out loud and said: what nonsense is this? What are you commanding us to do? We must not bow down to them, they must bow down to us!, Father looked at him and got very angry, then the clouds started appearing in the sky and started lightening, John said cool!, Luzie continued; he then moved towards Lucifer and said: my beloved creature why are you forsaking me? And he noticed that Lucifers color was changed by that time, he looked more darken and the feathers of his wings had turned black mostly, so Father said: what has happened to you Lucifer? Lucifer shout and said: what has happened to you huh? And lightening stroke more, he said: I look like you more than he does(Adam), I have unlimited powers as you have (God) I am an immortal too and no Angel can ever dare to stand on my way, so why should I bow down? God became very angry, he raised his voice and said: because I commanded you to do so, Lucifer laughed and said: this is my problem you just command when you feel weak, you use us as your servents, you throw us in the pathetic battles and when we loose you punish us by making such powerless creatures, I loved you more than all the Angels in here, I served you more than all f them, I did what you had commanded me to do so, but I will not do it anymore, as from now onwards I will no longer serve you, Fathers anger raised, the Heaven turned into Darkness, lightening stroke everywhere, Father shouted and said: you went to the forbidden kingdom without my permission? Lucifer laughed and said: isn't it getting boring for you sometimes that you know everything or know it even before it had happened? He then shouted and said: if you know everything then why are you letting those innocent souls to burn in that burning lake and pay no attention to it? Are we going to end like them? Are we now so useless for you that you make such creatures and tell us to bow down to them? I feel the one who must be judged and punish, is no one but you? You must be locked in that lake, Father shouted out loud the whole Heaven shook, we were all so much afraid and were holding each other very tight, Father shouted again and said: enough is enough, you have spoken more than your limit, he then said: can't you see that I made you first and gave you this kingdom so you could never feel sorrow, never feel trouble, never feel failed? Can't you see that what I have done was for the goodness of you and the rest? Can`t you understand that I have made humans to make us more responsible, more loved, more wanted? Are you jealous of them? I have made them so we can learn something from them as well, as they take their decisions themselves and need us to guide them at all time, Lucifer stretched his neck and said: I am jealous of them and the place you made for them, you adore them more that you adore us, you love them more than you love us, Father shouted and said: I love all my good creatures equally, Lucifer laughed said oh ya? I wish I served Darkness, at least he hasn't stop loving his followers, Father shouted louder and the Heaven shook again, said: Darkness he knows no love, he is no love, he has no love, how can you say such things while you everything? Lucifer raised his voice and said: I wish you would go to Hell and he would lead us instead of you, Fathers anger reached to its highest, he raised his right hand up and was about to strike the Lucifer but Gabriel ran and stood in front of Lucifer and said Father! Father! Please control your anger, he then turned around facing to Lucifer said: what are you doing brother, but Lucifer punched him in the face, the attack was too powerful for Gabriel to bear so he was thrown away, Lucifer then shouted and said: I want the Earth, I want to become to be the king of the Earth, God looked more angry, he shouted and said: it is done, I will take all your Holy powers from you, and also your holiness so you will never be able to enter this place again, Lucifer smiled and said: perfect! but I need my people to get released from the forbidden kingdom and my Master as well and I want them all to be sent to Earth, so that I will make my own army and will defeat you when the time is right, God said: nothing he took Lucifers powers and released the Darkness and the Evil army, I remember that day every well as the Heaven was covered by Darkness and a lot of scary noises, after releasing Darkness and the Evil army, father had sent them all to the Earth even though he loved his creation so much but he wanted to prove to Lucifer that he would never reject his beloved creatures of what they demand him to do, even though father knew this would cause serious problems in future but he still did what he thought was right.

Anyway after he went(Lucifer) everything went back to normal again, we forgot about what had happened in past and Gabriel was blessed by the highest power which made him the new leader of all the Angels. So one day as you know Father was walking in his kingdom and was playing with his humans and also teaching them about the things around them, for a while he left them alone as he was creating some other things, and when he went back he realised that Adam & Eve had betrayed him by eating the fruit of knowledge which was planned by Lucifer. He became furious, he called all the Angels, and Lucifer as well, he then looked at Lucifer and said: what have you done to my creatures, then he looked at the Adam and Eve and said: why have you forsaken me and listened to him(pointing towards Lucifer) we tried to make him to calm down but Father felt extremely disappointed and failed, meanwhile Lucifer laughed and said: this is just the beginning of what I will do to you at war, Father thought for a while and said: I will offer you a deal, If I become victorious in the battle by using the same powerless creatures and my Angels, I will lock you and your Evil army and Master in the burning lake of the fire for the rest of the eternity and if I fail you can have my position! Many of the Angels immediately left Father and joined Lucifer as they losed their faith by hearing such commitment but we who believed in him stood by his side, Lucifer laughed and said: very well, I will see you soon and will have your position sooner, for now bye and he went back to the Earth with the rest, after sometimes Father dropped Adam and Eve on Earth as they were no longer Holy to stay in Heaven, since then kept protecting the humans by sending his true Disciples, faithful souls and us to the Earth, and as you know he had sent his own son to save the world which he successfully did but still after even knowing the truth humans left moving on the right direction, and started doing the things they had desired and do desire, and now they have started believing in him (God.SED) just like they never heard or read any Holy messages or books.

John was chewing his nails again, he said: Wow man! Wow man!, such a tragedy, I gotta ask you this question too, what`s the story behind the Evil and Devil? Luzie replied: they are Lucifers sons, the darkness inside of them is unimaginable as they have their Fathers unholy blood moreover, they are all blessed by the unholy powers from Darkness, it is impossible for any ordinary Angel to fight against them and defeat them. The only one who can fight against them is The leader, John said: Gabriel! Luzie replied: yes of course but he himself can not fight against Lucifer as Lucifer has still the blood that he had received from Father which is the Holy Spirit itself and moreover he has the unholy power of Darkness too which makes him a very powerful creature, we Angels know this truth that we will not be able to defeat Lucifer by our own, we might be able to defeat the sons of him through Gabriel but for defeating him we will need fathers blessings again which will make him disappointed again, but there is a prophesy in the Heaven, John said: wow! You guys have prophesies too? Luzie nodded her head and said: of course we have, and it says a man will have the powers of the highest holiness and through the Seven Golden Arrows of termination; he will give an end to the war and make us victorious! But by using the Arrows he will give an end to his existence, not only on this planet but for the eternity as well, John said: what you mean? she replied: I mean he will be gone from the history of existence, John said: but Father will make him again huh? Luzie put her hed down and said: we hope, and pray for that.

After awhile of thinking John said: so who is the blessed one, the in charge of these Arrows? Luzie looked at him and said: you really don't know? And then touched Johns Holy Sign and said: it is you Johnny!, John almost perished, his tongue stopped moving, his voice wasn't coming out anymore, weakly said: me? Me? But how will it be possible? Luzie held his hands tightly and said: Johnny this is what has been told to us according to the prophecy, sometimes, some things must happen and we have no control over them but you must remember if happenings bring glory to Father then it is worthy to do anything for him, do you understand this? John nodded his head and he went to the fridge opened its door, took two sandwiches out and brought them to the place where they were sitting, and pushed one of them close to Luzie and said: please eat Angel I mean Luzie, but Luzie nodded her head and said: the time has come for me to go, I will dine with my family members when I reach home, John swallowed the food inside his mouth and said: you need to go now what time is it? He then turned around and looked at the clock on the wall and noticed that it had crossed 12:00am then he looked at Luzie and said: but I will be all alone, what will I do without you? I know that I am a grown man, but I will need your help, you are the only family that I have, can't you go after some days? Or maybe next week? I don't know maybe next year? Luzie smiled and cleaned her tears, her tears were as shiny as a rare Jewel, she looked at John and said, I need to go John, I miss my family as much as you will miss me, and then a shiny light appeared in the room which made the whole place very bright and the time stopped for awhile, the clock stopped ticking, even the Mosquito which was about to sting John was hanging in the air, she said: oppss! I guess the old Nanny has to go now!, John couldn't control himself and his tears kept falling down, in a very shivering voice he said: I won't say good bye, because I will see you soon and I will have you in my heart forever, Luzie while standing at the middle of the bright light said: indeed, and started getting invisible, and while getting invisible said: I love you Johnny and disappeared. Some hours passed, and John was just sitting alone in the kitchen deeply thinking then he went to the dark dining room and stood near the fire place and looked at the pictures which were standing on it, his tears were falling, he realised that Luzie had been unusually glowing in each pictures and he never paid enough attention to it, moreover the shadow of her wings was visible in most of the places that they were standing, he remembered the first time he wanted to thigh his shoe laces and how Luzie thought him to do so,he remembered that one day back in his school, the teacher of the class scolded all the students as she was a very picky one but John called Luzie and she took care of the teacher, and since then the teacher became the students best friend which made John a popular boy in the school as students thought he had a Super Nanny, he then losed himself, he went to his room, fell on the bed, he never felt that alone in his entire life, he had some sort of pain, the pain of insecurity, he felt what would happen next? Who would knock his door every single day and bring his breakfast and who would be there when he would face difficulties? Who would give him advice and guide him? He knew Sara would always stand by his side, but no one could fill the empty space of Luzies absence for him, he cried and cried until he fell asleep.

After sometimes he again got the same nightmare that he used to get when he was a teenager, in the nightmare, he always saw Sara was screaming for help, she was surrounded by people who did not have eyes, they had hands of the cat and feet of the horse, they were laughing out loud like the clowns at circus, he saw himself trying to save her and help her but he couldn't do, how much he tried to reach to Sara it looked like he was moving more far from her, while he was dreaming he rolled on his bed and fell down from it, and he quickly woke up and while chanting looked at the clock, it just crossed 3:00am, so he turned on the light and started praying: Heavenly Father, I adore you for your love, mercy, and the blessings that you have always given to me, so many things have happened and it is so much tough for me to handle myself and control myself, I keep having these horrible nightmares every often which truly makes me terrified and very uncomfortable, I don't know what to do Father, please show me the way, please Father take care of Sara if something terrible is going to happen to her, father I request you to help everyone in the world as well, as we humans may have forgotten about your glory and power but you never forget any one of us as we are your creatures and to save our souls, we will always need your blessings, I love you so much Father, and I will do anything that I can to stop Evil and make this place a better place until your Holy son comes and bless us all, I pray all of these in the name of the glory of your Holy son . . . Amen!

He then went to the bathroom, washed his face, he then went back to the bedroom, grabbed the glass of water which was on his desk, drank some water, while drinking he realised that he didn't put the glass on the desk, so he smiled and said: I hope that I see you soon. And then he slept

After awhile he had another nightmare, he saw himself standing on a melting ground, and as far as he could was burning fire and several Angels who were fighting with Demons around him, he looked at himself and saw he looked like a standing wolf, covered by black long hair and was holding up something by his right hand, he looked up and realised he was holding an Angel from his throat, he couldn't see the Angels face but he realised that he was fighting against the Angels not for them, and he fell off the bed again, this time he was not only chanting but also sweating very much, he looked at the clock and saw it was 7:00am, he got himself together and opened the doors of balcony to get some fresh air, he had some unusual feeling, he realised that something worse was going to happen soon, not only to him and Sara but to whole the world, as in his dream he saw Angels fighting against Demons which meant the end of the world.

Then he went to bathroom, took a warm shower, brushed his teeth, and while drying his hair, with a navy color towel he came out, he then combed his hair, he wore a simple light blue T-shirt which did not have God.SED picture on it, he wore another JoJo, and wore comfortable shoes too, he decided not to go to hospital that day and instead take Sara out and give her a very good time as he has some bad feelings about his future with Sara, so he wanted to make the best of the days while he would be with Sara, he then opened his laptop to check his e-mails and saw he had many messages in his inbox, he opened them one by one and read, they where mostly from Sara, in some she wrote, switch your phone on, in some I love you sweet heart, in some I miss you, in some call me please and many other words, and while calling Sara he opened a message which didn't have any address on it but before he read it, Sara picked his call and pretended like she didn't know him and said: who is this? John replied: this is your future husband who wants to take you to Parasis* (it was the new name of Paris) today, to give you some good time, she screamed really!? Really!? John said: yes of course, he looked at the clock and said: I will pick you up in around 20minutes okay? Sara screamed again and said: but I haven't any good cloths with me!, John replied: this life isn't about good cloths or manmade stuff sweat heart but don't worry, I'll take care of it, so after his conversation was over he wanted to open the unknown message but he told to himself that he would read it later, and then opened his bedrooms door and said: loudly good morning! Where is my honey Nanny? But suddenly remembered that there was no Nanny any longer, so disappointed went to kitchen and stood stunned, there was a plate on the table on which there were two roasted eggs, three pieces of white bread, a glass of orange juice and also there was a red Rose which was laying beside the plate on the table, John smiled and said: I wasted all those tears last night for nothing? He looked up and said: you didn't tell me you would take care of me like this, well thank you so much your highness, and while eating he said: everyone needs a Nanny like mine, boy! She is the best. When his eating was over, he washed the dishes as quick as he could, took whatever he needed and put them in a bag, then locked the doors and while he was about to walk away from the house, he noticed an unusual mail on the foot-path on which there was no address, he got a little bit suspicious as he had received some crazy unknown messages since morning, he put the mail in his bag and after getting a taxi he went towards Michelle's house(actually since Saras father died in a very horrible car accident, Sara and John stopped moving around by driving a car or riding a bike).

After awhile he reached to the building where Michelle was living at, it was a circular shape building which was looking like a scoop of ice cream, he called Sara and told her to go down, as he didn't like to go to Michelle's house, Michelle was a nice person but because he went to God.SED and received blessings to get woman breast and bottom, John had stopped trusting him ever since.

Sara came down and hugged John then sat in the Taxi which looked like a large boat with wheels, then said: bye to Michelle who was standing at the door of the building, but John said no words and sat in the car, Michelle waved his hand and said: bye sister, have fun with your virgin boy friend, then John and Sara went from there.

Michelle took a deep breath, looked around but before, he entered into the building he heard a Virgin Collector calling him, he stood stunned and he got very scared, a Virgin Collector who was smoking came forward and said: how about you inviting me inside? Michelle started shaking, he replied: okay! Do you wanna have good time sugar, the virgin Collector smiled very evilly and said: indeed, and by pushing Michelle, they went inside the building.

Meanwhile John and Sara reached to the SED-Loves-Connection which was the name of the super fast train which would go anywhere around the world within few hours or even seconds, so John bought two tickets in

Private Class Cabin, and while they were talking, they sat in it and within a very short time the train started moving. Sara looked at John and said: what have you been up to last night that you forgot all about me huh? John looked down and said: Nanny left! Sara's eyes opened widely and she immediately said: what? When? How? Why? Did she tell you? John looked at her (very upset) then said: ya she told me but the way she went, is just beyond imagination to talk about it, Sara got suspicious, and said: at least she could call me and say good bye, John said: she hasn't gone very far but the place she went is indeed far from us, after sometimes Sara took a deep breath and said: I hope she is happy where she is! Then she looked at John in a naughty way and said: guess what?, I slept with Michelle last night, the words just blew a bomb in Johns mind, he raised his voice and said: have you gone mad? You slept with a half man half woman man? What do you want me to say now that I can trust you and will live with you? The other people who were hearing him had started clapping and cheering, they said: praise the God.SED who makes man into a woman and a woman into a man, Sara laughed out loud, she sat beside John kissed him on the lips and said: I slept on her bed, while wearing my pants and your T-shirt, John looked at her and said: it wasn't funny you know that? Sara laughed and said: it's good to see you possessive sometimes as we girls like our man to get jealous of what we do so they protect us more, John replied: (in a very charming way) you don't know how tough we may get while dwelling and laughed, Sara pinched him and said: you naughty boy behave (in a very round British accent), while talking the cabin hostess came and gave them food to eat and she went out.

The journey between the Peace Land to Parisis was about 5 hours; as the train was moving with an extra ordinary speed, mean while Sara had fallen asleep, and was leaning her head on Johns shoulder. John looked out the window at the things and the places where they were crossing from, he noticed that nothing was right, everything was changed indeed but got worse, as far as he could see was the picture of crime, injustice, discrimination, unfaithfulness, no one respect no one anymore, it was like people were living in a hypnotized and senseless world, then John looked at Sara, she was a pure British girl, having brown hair, blue eyes, fair skin, sharp face, she was about 175cm tall, having good physics as she used to do jogging a lot, while he was looking at her he had a flash back, he remembered the first time that he met Sara, they were in Turkey, she was being chased by a crazy man and John rescued her from him, after that day onwards they were always together. Saras father was from England, he died in a horrible car crash while he was dropping Sara back to their home, and the strange part about their lives was that Saras mother was too died while giving birth to her, as John heard Saras mother was a Turkish woman and as Sara told him she had her mother`s hair and lips. She had gone through so much problems as well which made John to love her more as he believed she was very mature than what she looked.

After Sara's father died, the responsibility of her life fell in the hands of Luzie, which she really had taken care of it. Sara and John both wanted to become Artists, they loved to perform when they were young so they were always busy in Acting and Drama, they were nominated for the best students and the best couples during their Educational years, she wasn't believing in Christ at the beginning but slowly, slowly she started believing and became a Christian by going to the church regularly with John, she was a very honest girl, very kind and loving, she did care about the things happening around her because she went trough so much difficulties in her life which made her to become very tough in all the situations that she used to be at, she was Johns soul mate, for this John was completely sure as he could feel her spiritually.

While thinking about this, he looked outside of window again, and he took a deep breath he thought several God believing people were murdered or taken away, Churches, Mosques, Temples and several other Holy places were all evacuated by the army of God.SED, while looking he felt to go and wash his face, he slowly put Sara's head on the sofa where they were sitting on it and went to the washroom, when he was washing his face, he heard some cheering, it was like some people were clapping and celebrating, he then dried his face by a towel, and slowly went out from the room, and stood stunned, an old topless man was removing a teenage girls cloths off, the strange part was that the girl was reading a magazine on which it was written how to become a prostitute, John became very angry, he felt the power inside him again but this time he controlled it in his hands, people around the place were involved in physical activities and were having fun, suddenly the girl screamed very loud and said: I will have your children in me so John realised that she was under influence of some Evil powers, not only her but also the rest of the people, so he raised his right hand up, he could feel the energy rushing towards his hand, and then he shouted and said: by the power of my Father I command this place to be cleaned up from all the Evil Spirits, and he felt the energy was released from his hand and body, the energy waves were blown into the cabin and acted like an explosion towards Johns body, John flew in the air and was thrown back, when he opened his eyes again, he saw the girl who screamed and the rest of the people were standing around him and were looking at him, he noticed the girl had covered herself with a blanket and the old man was looking very ashamed, a black man grabbed his hand and said: stand up brother, you saved us all, John stood up weakly and said: I haven't, our Father did, then the girl who was being stripped off by the old man hugged John and said: thank you for letting us remember him, suddenly Sara shouted and said: what on Earth is happening here? John immediately turned around and said: nothing just amm! just, Sara raised her voice up and said: get back in here Mr. Seven (whenever she used to get angry, she used to speak with a very round British accent), John looked at the passengers and said: I believe something big is going to happen soon, so pray that Father bless us all and have mercy on us, and went in the room and Sara shut the door. She was stepping her right foot up and down and looked very angry, John said: I can explain, Sara started removing her cloth, John shocked and said: what are you doing? Sara replied: you like naked women, so have me instead of them!, John rushed to her and held her hands then said: it is true, I am the one who must be blamed but I told you that I can explain everything but I don't want today be the day of explanation, but Sara looked upset as she felt there was something that John was hiding from her.

After couple of hours, they had reached to Paris, the city was completely changed, the colors, the way of wearing cloths, the way of eating, everything was simply changed, even the color of Ifel tower was changed into pink, but it was normal for the people walking around there as the whole world was changed as well.

Sara never looked that happy before, but she was hiding herself behind Johns back as the clothes which she was wearing were not as stylish as the people around, John shook her hand and said: you don't need to be shy as if you are wearing simple green T-shirt and yellow color simple Jeans, I didn't bring you here to think about these, I brought you here to feel special of being different from everyone around you, who have forgotten the truth about their lives and this world, Sara looked at him and said: have you ever thought that you advice me so much Mr. Seven?, John stopped and said: because you don't know how much I love you, and how much I want you to be relaxed about the things that you have and you don't, Sara put her fingers on Johns lips and said: I know my future husband, but I am hungry now Johnny, treat me well today please!(she started blinking while making a childish face), John kissed her forehead and said: indeed I will my Queen, so they went to a restaurant. The name of the restaurant was Eat & Forget, after reading the strange name of the restaurant, John felt very much suspicious but he didn't want to ruin the day by saying not to go here and there, so they both entered inside the restaurant.

It was a beautiful restaurant, all the tables were in round shape, made by metal, and were covered by red color table sheets, the chairs were too made by metal and they were also in round shape, the walls were painted by different colors and had many large spots on them. The floor was in green color and was made from metal as well. And there were several pictures of God.SED hanging on all over the place, even there was a large statue of him standing right middle of the restaurant, from which a very clean water was flowing out side, on the statue it was written, Drink The Holy Water and forget About Your Miseries, the words gave John, an awaking alarm as it looked suspicious to him, but he felt it wasn't a big deal to be suspicious about it so he started looking around while Sara was checking the menu out to order food for them. A waitress came forward, she looked like she came back from a battle, she looked very unclean and dirty, she wore a large hat on her head, and was wearing a tore ballerinas cloth on which there was spots of blood, and was standing with bare feet, John looked at her green eyes, there was so much pain and sorrow in them, John looked at Sara, she was busy thinking, making some childish noises and wasn't able to decide, John smiled and said: how about, Love-Spaghetti*(Love-Spaghetti was the name of a Meal in which the Spaghettis were in pink color and were covered by many strawberries),Sara nodded her head and said: perfect, she then looked at the waitress and said: we`ll have a large plate of Spaghettis and for the drink, the waitress interrupted her speaking by saying, we have no drinks in here, you can have free Holy Water which taste like red wine, Sara looked at John then very doubtfully said: okay! We may have that as well later on. When the waitress went, Sara looked at John and Said: this place is a little bit strange isn't it? John nodded his head and said: the whole world is strange now then he looked out of the window which was beside him, while looking at people he noticed a Pigeon which was flying towards him, he thought the Pigeon will hit the window but the Pigeon sat near the window and looked at John straight in his eyes, for a moment John thought

Luzie was looking at him so he got alerted and turned his face and started paying attention to the people sitting in the restaurant. He noticed a father was drinking the Holy Water and was hitting his child in the face, there was a P.SED member in the restaurant who was squeezing a woman`s legs and was trying to get her cloths off, he noticed there were a lot of people around the statue of God.SED and were drinking the water wildly, he looked at the others and saw some people were doing the exact thing that the other were doing, it looked like a part of time was repeating again and again, then he heard a waitress saying to a new comers that whether they wanted some Holy Water or not, John kept looking at the new customers, the waitress went near the statues poured two glassed from the water and gave it to the new customers, the customers drank the water and turned crazy, they started kissing each other wildly and had started removing their cloths and screaming which even got Saras attention, by seeing these things John realised the place was cursed, from the water to its food, so he fell on the floor and pretended like he had a very bad stomachache, some waitresses came forward and told him to drink water but he looked at Sara and said: take me out of here, I have to go to Red People*(Red People were doctors who were in charge of healing people while walking around the city), Sara while being really upset and worried took him out of there, after awhile of walking and getting far from the place, John looked at her and said: how was my acting? Sara got very angry and said: what is with you Mr. Seven? Why have you taken me this far if you want to ruin the day like this? John was shocked, he asked: haven't you seen what was going on in the restaurant? Haven't you seen how people were behaving? Sara looked at him just like he was crazy or something, and then said: John I am sure this strange behaviour of yours doesn't have any link with Nannys leaving? While Sara was complaining, John heard some unusual noises, he looked around, he smelled a very bad smell too, and he quickly held Sara's hand and took her to an empty street then moved her towards the wall of a building and started touching Sara's body, Sara turned red and said: have you gone mad? Do you want to do it right here? John was still touching her, Sara smiled and hugged John and said: wow! finally! I have been waiting for this moment for a long time, don't worry about the people around us, they will adore us, John started touching and feeling Sara's bottom, Sara smiled closed her eyes and said: I am all yours my love, and started kissing Johns lips, John moved his head near Sara's ear and said: sweetie, I was just searching for the cross that I gave you, remember we are not yet married, Sara opened her eyes, she looked extremely shied and angry, she pushed John back and said: you know what John? I may leave you, I just can't bear this anymore, John while holding the golden cross, hugged Sara and said: don't you dare saying that again! What happens if we don't have sex? What happens if I behave strange just to protect you? Don't you believe in me anymore Sara? Why do you need me to have biological contact with you to prove that I love you, he then looked around and said: I know what to do to prove it, John ran and stood middle of the street and shouted out loud: all of you people look at me, some did some didn't, he shout out loud: I said look at me, many people looked and many came forward to see what was happening? John pointed his finger towards Sara and shouted: I love that woman standing right there, Sara wasn't believing of what she was hearing, John Shouted: I love her so much, I can go beyond the universe for that single lady right there, people started cheering for him, I will do anything to keep her safe and I will fight for her with anyone who stands on my way! People were cheering and clapping for him, Sara was coming forward slowly and she looked very shy, John Shouted and said: she is my soul mate and I will adore her as a rare Jewel, people went crazy by hearing the words, many girls perished right away, meanwhile Sara came and stood beside John, John said: God has blessed me with her and I will never leave her alone and let her leave me alone for my heart doesn't beat without having her, people started cheering for them very loudly which made some

P.SED members suspicious but because he was talking about love they let him continue, John then turned, facing towards Sara and kissed her as best as he could, no one was standing without cheering for them, many started kissing too, the crowd around them went crazy.

After awhile, John stopped kissing Sara, and while being almost worshiped by the people around him, he started walking towards some other shops, Sara was speechless, she couldn't believe the thing that John has done, so she seemed really proud of him, while walking John looked up and in his heart said: Father forgive me if I have committed adultery but I do want to save her and not let her to be disappointed in me as I love her so much, I know you know what I am doing as my life is in your hands, please forgive us for the sins that we commit, while he was praying Sara looked at him and said: I wanna go home Johnny, John (doubtfully) said: home? she said: ya I have had what I came here for, so let's go home and eat food there, John smiled and said: as you command my lady, so from there they went to the SED-Loves-Connection train and went to home. The house was truly empty and very silent without Luzie, Sara told to John that she wanted to take a shower and expected him to cook for her, so she went upstairs. John stretched his back a bit and then washed his hands and face in the sink and while drying them by some tissue paper he opened the fridge, he couldn't believe of what he was looking at, a large plate full of Love-Spaghetti was there, covered by several strawberries, John couldn't be happier than that moment, he looked up and said: I love you Luzie, thank you for saving my day, he took the plate out and then removed a jar full of grape juice too, and put them on the table, put two large candles with their stands on the table, he also spread some Red Rose leaves on the table as well and turned off the light, the place looked beautiful and very romantic, he then sat behind a chair and started playing with flame of the candle, while playing he remembered about the unusual mail that he received in the morning, so he went and brought his bag and took the mail out of it, he opened the letter, it was from Luzie she just had written try not to leave Peace land as today is not favourable for you two, he just smiled and put the letter back in the bag, while he was putting the letter back, he heard that Sara was coming down stairs so he quickly took the plate and put it in the microwave to make it warm, he turned around and the whole world roamed around his head, Sara was standing at the door way, she was wet, and had John`s bath towel around her, Johns heart started beating faster, it was like he wanted to roar his life out, Sara looked at him in a very naughty way and said what? She then lowered her voice and said: do you like of what you see? John made a horse sound and said: who wouldn't like it? We must get married soon! Sara nodded and said: but when? While John was removing the plate out of the microwave, said: even now we can get married, I can look at sky say Father I love this girl she loves me back we know we are meant for each other and by the power vested in you we get married as easy as that but Sara I don't think so our faith is enough for such commitment yet, Sara looked at him made some faces and said maybe your faith is not enough in me but mine is a 100% for you Mr. Seven, John smiled and said: I know, do you remember when we were 17 and 18 we decided to get married we even went to the church but unfortunately you got angry with the Pastor who delayed the ceremony and you just punched the innocent man in the face, Sara smiled, I know you are a 100% faithful lady, but he took a deep breath, I believe something big is going to happen soon, so I feel we better wait for a longer time your highness!, I know we are both humans and because of some biological developments we need to start getting involved in practicing it too but believe me Sara, having sex is completely different from love, you see these days people say let's make love, for Heavens sake the word is sex not love, love is what Jesus Christ showed and gave to us, love is a powerful energy that makes the impossible possible, love is like doing the things you think that you can not do, to make someone feel better, meanwhile Sara moved forward and forward, then stood on Johns feet and looked in the eyes of John and said: do you know you talk too much?, don't make me perish on this floor because of hunger, John smiled then said: as you command my lady, and they started eating the food, and kept talking middle of the conversation, some idea hit Johns head, he told to Sara that he wanted to do an experiment on Sara so after finishing the meal, they washed the dishes, and then John took Sara to his room, Sara looked much more dry now but still had nothing on except the towel, which she was wrapped in it. So she went towards Johns closet to take some cloth out to wear but John told her not to, he even told her to take off the towel as well. Sara started looking at him in a very strange way, she said: are you drunk? Was something in the food? John replied: I will get all my clothes off as well but I will not be looking at your body as it is written that we must not see some ones nakedness until we are married, so I want you to do the same, Sara was a bit shocked but she trusted John very much, so while they were naked john told her to lay on the bed, and she did, the John took a deep breath and said: here we go. He told to Sara to start imagining that they were about to have sex, which gave a push to Sara's mind, he told her to imagine he was at the top of her body and was kissing her lips, Sara started getting red, john said: imagine that I am kissing your body right now and holding your hand up tight, Sara started smiling, he then said: imagine my hand is going somewhere around your treasure, Sara laughed, imagine we are about to reach to the final stage of the process but you hear a voice, you hear some kid is crying out loud on the street so you stand up to see what is going on, so you stand and go towards the balcony and see yes a small boy is getting beaten by several wild people with no reason, Sara crossed her eye brows into each other, John said: imagine the kid is telling the truth about something that he hasn't done but people aren't believing, and now imagine I am kissing your arms and playing with your body, imagine you see the kid being harshly beaten and after sometimes imagine falls on the ground and perishes, and the people who were chasing him go away, now decision is yours! Will you go to the kid to help him up and save his life or will you turn around and have wild sex with me, suddenly a blanket was thrown on John, he opened his eyes saw Sara was sitting at his chair, wearing his pyjamas and was combing her hair, then she said: you made your point my future husband, John covered himself by the blanket and said: well done Mrs. Future Seven, you have passed your test, Sara then put the comb down and said: you could simply tell me in a very short way and I would obey, John took a deep breath and said: I have done the same thing that the lord had done to make people realise the truth but they were not as understandable and faithful as you are so we ended up reaching to this dark age. He(Jesus Christ)was perished like that little boy and even died for our sins but people were busy doing other stuffs so much that they forgot to see what jewel was getting broken, and now we all have to pay the price, Sara removed comfortable home cloths out of the closet and went to John, then gave them to him and said: you could teach these things you know that? And you better take a shower as you look very tired; until you come out I will prepare some snacks okay? Then she went downstairs.

John took a deep breath and actually felt good about the thing that he had done and became very proud of Sara that she did not fail in the experiment, so he went to the bathroom, after he took shower, he decided to shave his beards as well, as they looked not very proper. He then removed his shaving razor out of the bathroom cabinet, put it on the sink and when he closed the door of the cabinet, he was just terrified. He didn't know what to do, he couldn't even move as his body was iced, there was a supernatural image at the mirror of the cabinet, it was Johns face but half of it was a Demon face behind whom there was burning fire and the half of the face was the face of an Angel behind whom there was a blue sky, John just closed his eyes and said: Father please help me! and help Sara let us be able to keep ourselves on the right and the good side, don't leave our hands

Father as we need you more than ever. He then quickly shaved and after washing his face and cleaning it, he went to Sara. The sitting room was lighten by the light of the T.V and the rest was dark, Sara was sitting on the black leather sofa and was watching the news channel, John went near her and sat on the sofa, there was a huge oval shape bowl in front of the sofa on the table in which there was Crazy-Jumpers*(new name of Pop Corn), by seeing Johns face, Sara immediately asked: what is wrong? Why do you look very terrified huh? And then started playing with Johns hair, John looked at her in the eyes and said: this is the time that I have to tell you about a very important matter!, Sara nodded her head and said: tell me, John said: it won't be easy for you to accept or believe in it but you need to trust me in this, Sara nodded her head again, John took a deep breath and said: my mother is an Angel, and I am half Angel as well, Sara just blinked, John told her about all the supernatural incidents that happened to him during his life time until the same day, after telling her everything, he said: Sara I feel the lord is going to come sooner that we think, I just don't feel it, I believe in it, he said: I am sure something bad is going to happen soon, we must be aware of everything that is going on around us, he then held Saras hands and asked do you believe in the lord? Sara nodded her head and said: I not only believe in him but also the things you are telling me, and suddenly the whole house shook, and a very bright light appeared in the room which forced Sara and John to close their eyes, then John heard Luzies voice he barely opened his eyes and simply shocked, Luzie was in front of him and looked very angry, Sara screamed and hid behind John, John said:(happily) hi, welcome back, I didn't know I would see you so soon, then he looked at Sara and said: let me introduce her to you, this is Luzie, our old Nanny, Luzie (by loud voice) said: she is not worthy to know anything about me!, John looked at her in a very doubtful way and said: but . . . Luzie shouted: she is not the one who she pretends that she is!, she doesn't believe in light and neither you John!, she believes in nothing except the things she sees! She then asked: will you sacrifice yourself for her John? Tell me will you? John didn't know what was going on, he looked at Sara who looked very scared and said: if I have to yes I will, Luzie became more angry and shouted: will you go to Hell because of saving such faithless creatures life?, John started looking serious and a bit angry, he said: what is with you Luzie?, what faithless? What are you talking about? I don't understand anything luzie!, luzie calmed down and said: she (Sara) doesn't hear us anymore as the time has stopped from going forward, she then looked at John and said: the war has already begun, this is the final time that I will see you on Earth, and maybe the last time that I see you at all, John said: what you mean huh? Luzie replied: the Satan's army has become very powerful and are ready to take over the world, which they will do soon, we have our army ready and the lord is about to come soon to take the souls who have the Heavenly Sign and after that the battle will began, John whatever you do will be your choice so do not make any decisions without thinking before it okay? John looked very confused and didn't know what to say. Luzie then said: John Father blesses and protects the one who loves him and pray to get connected to him, but the one who is not connected will not be saved, it doesn't matter what she or he does, will not be saved! but you have the power to make decision after decisions and change your future at any moment as you want, she then came closer and said john don't make any foolish decision as we will need you in our army, while she was speaking a breaking news was going on, on the T.V, the reporter was giving the latest information of the day about God.SED, (the reporter was wearing a black robe and looked very pale, she was bald and on her head there was a picture of God.SED which was tattooed.)

The reporter had reported that God.SED has been transformed into his final stage of power and glory, Luzie wasn't looking just said: John have you started practicing your powers? John while looking at T.V replied: yes I . . . luzie interrupted saying have you started seeing the truth about people's real image, John said: I don't know how should I do it? Luzie smiled and said: I wonder how will you save the world? John while looking at T.V in which the images of God.SED were being showed, said: excuse me! I didn't hear you properly! What did you say?, Luzie shook her wings and said: I wonder . . . suddenly John said: did you see that? Luzie turned around and saw that God.SED had transformed into a 2.30m man, very fair, having brownish hair, blue eyes, very muscular, wearing an old style Roman cloth and was standing at the top of his pillar, several other P.SED members and Sky eyes*(Sky eyes were tall reddish new protective units, they were around 190cm tall, very muscular, all were bald and having shades at all time, the were wearing wine color tight leather cloths and were in charge of protecting the people and God.SED by flying in sky through their Fankos* Fankos were the flying vehicles which only were being used by Sky eyes, the vehicles could fly with a very high speed, they looked like a big flying bat, if there would an emergency which was more dangerous than the normal Crimes and Protests, these protectors would rush to the place immediately, but till that day there never been such dangerous situation which the P.SED members couldn't handle so, Sky eyes were normally flying from country to country and having their own checking).

Luzie looked at John and asked: can't you still see anything?, John said: no? And quickly said: hey if the time has stopped then how this news channel . . . he then said: oh! I see everything now, John couldn't believe that all these years he was living under such Evil power.

John could see the truth, as he started concentrating and using his Holy powers, he saw the real image of God.SED, he saw a very tall, muscular Monster was standing right at the pillar, he looked like a Bat which had figure of a man, he had large black wings with no feathers, he had a face of a man, long stretched eyes, ears of cat, teeth of a lion, he looked like a human who turned into a large Bat, he had two large horns as well, he had a long tail as well, his nails were very long and his hands looked like the claws of a lion, he was laughing and from his mouth a black liquid was flowing out, on his back there was another Monster, he looked very similar to the first Monster except he was shorter, fatter and smaller as well, he was holding himself on the bigger Monster and was licking his ear, John looked at the other creatures around them, the P.SED members were Demons, and had terrifying image, but the Sky eyes were burning Beasts, they had no hairs on their body, and from top to toes were covered by a weak flame, they had no eyes, no ears, but a very large mouth with large number of teeth, they didn't have nose as well instead they had two large holes on their face which worked as their nose, their vehicles were flying Demons, they looked like large bats but having the face of humans.

John looked at the Temple, it wasn't a Temple, it was a Dungeon, and from every parts of it fire flames were boosting out. It was constructed like two open hands which were attached to each other and from the center of them several Demons were moving out.

John closed his eyes slowly and opened them again, then he looked at luzie and asked:, how long do we have? Luzie (very sorrowfully) said: shorter than you imagine, she then looked at Sara and said: she won't enter the heaven, (John became angry), she said: I feel your anger, your love for her, you do care for her but you cannot have her and light both, luzie said: she will not come with you, John became more angry, she said; she will stay on Earth and find her mother and you will not be able to do anything, John started turning into red color and closed his fingers, Luzie said: you will not need her, John could not control himself and shout: enough!, enough now! enough, his sign started shining, and suddenly a very powerful energy waves was released from him, the whole house turned into a mess, but this time John didn't move into any where as he was controlling himself, he Shouted and said I will do anything to save her soul, even if I go to Hell for her sake, Luzie smiled and said: the future can not be changed but yours can be, (she smiled) and said: you have really learnt to control your powers and even learnt how to shout on me!, John felt very bad for a moment, he didn't believe of what he had done, he put his head down and said: forgive me for my rudeness, it's just . . . Luzie(with a very calm voice said): I know you John, I grew you up, but this is your love and passion which make you do the things you don't want to, you prefer to go to Hell and turn your back on your father to save a girl who even doesn't believe in him? John said: in the scripture is written saving a soul is much more important than doing anything in this world, I never turned and will never turn my back on my Father, but I will save Sara, this is my promise!, Luzie seemed upset, she turned around, and said: no one knows what you will do next except the Father, I wish you don't take a wrong decision, she then slowly said: I wish I could show you, a part of what happened to us before the creation, then she opened her wings, A very bright light shined in the room, and she got disappeared, John was closing his eyes as the light was so much bright and unbearable, when he opened his eyes, saw himself on his bed. He looked around furiously and looked at the clock, it was sharp 7:00am again, he heard some noises coming from downstairs, he got up, and went close to the entering door and listened, Sara was singing and cooking as the sounds of cutting and plates were being heard by John. He couldn't concentrate, he tried to look at something and concentrate but he couldn't as so many thoughts were going on in his mind, he was thinking about the things Luzie told him last night, he then took a deep breath and closed his eyes and prayed, (Heavenly Father, I adore you for giving me the chance of living on your creation again, and be safe and healthy, Father! I have no control on the things which are about to happen in future, I have no plans and no idea of how it may look, but I know that impossible is possible for you, and if you want you can change any fortunes, Father I beg you to have mercy on me and Sara and give us a chance to be saved through your holiness as we are nothing without you, he then opened his eyes and Said: Father give me the power to make the impossible possible, use me for your purpose and let me make you proud, I pray these in the name of your Holy son Amen!, he then took his towel and went to take a shower.

While taking shower, he remembered of the energy which was released from him last night, and the way he controlled it, so he stood still and focused, he felt the energy in his body again, he focused more and started releasing it slowly, he never felt like that before, he looked at himself and saw he was glowing, a very hallow layer had appeared around him and was rotating around his body, he focused more and the layer appeared brighter and brighter, he looked around and realised that he was faster than the time, the drops of water which were flowing down from the shower, were moving very slowly, he even could touch them even before they fall, and suddenly Sara knocked the door, John losed his concentration, and the energy was blown from him into the walls and into the things which were in the bathroom, everything broke, the walls cracked, the tub broke from the middle, the pipes came out and the water started spreading everywhere, Sara screamed: what is going on in there and she opened the door, John was covering himself with the bath curtains, Sara said: what on earth happened here? Are you a Terrorist? What was that explosion? John while trying to control the water which was coming out from the pipe said: I can explain everything!, Sara while looking suspiciously and shocked said: you better, I am going to call the P.SED to come and fix this place up, but John interrupted her speaking by saying no! no! Just wait I will fix this place myself just let me come out of here, Sara said: okay come out then, John made some faces and said: Jesus Christ Sara, you know you should . . . Sara interrupted by saying: I should not see any ones nakedness bla bla and she shut the door, John sat in the tub and felt tired, he then closed his eyes, and kept repeating these words: as impossible is possible if I just believe, and after few seconds, he felt his energy level was at the top of it, he then opened his eyes and the whole bathroom was fixed, John smiled(naughtily) and said: hey boy! This is some serious shit I got in me, I mean serious power I got, thank you Father, he then dried up, wore some simple cloths and went downstairs.

Sara was cooking some food, and was cutting couple of tomatoes, she looked very cute as she had two small ponies on her head, she was wearing a light blue T-shirt, and a very nice lemon color pant on which there was small picture of God.SED, John slowly stood behind her and then kissed her cheek, Sara screamed turned around and said: are you crazy? I could cut myself!, John looked at her and then kissed her on the lips, Sara was amazed and a bit shocked too, but she was carried on, John then said: I wanna take you to get some Chocó koko*(name of the chocolate shakes and drinks which was very popular in those days), Sara smiled and said: but I cooked for you, John kissed her again and said: I'll eat it with my whole soul, and then hugged Sara very tightly, Sara hugged him back and said: what is wrong John? John looked at her and said: can't I hug my future wife as much as I want? Sara looked at him suspiciously and said: but you never used too kiss me so much and now hugging me, and hey what about the mess upstairs? John kissed her again and asked: what would have happened if we leave it just like that? What would have happened if we leave everything and go to Meat land(new name of Australia) or we go to Iceland(new name of North pole), how long are we going to live that we think about everything all the time? aren't we humans? Aren't we the most precious creatures of Father? He then hugged Sara again, Sara became serious and said: what is with you Johnny? Are you hiding something from me? You sound like Death, I don't like that!, John looked at her in the eye and said: Sara we humans have done everything according to our taste and desire, and never looked back to see what really we had done, we made some wrong choices, we tried to take a short cut to reach to the source sooner but we never reached, something big is going to happen! Bigger than all the incidents that you have seen, look!, he stepped back and started concentrating and the layer came to appearance, the knife was dropped from Sara's hand, she was shocked and amazed and afraid, she could feel the power that she never felt before, then John controlled himself and said: I am one of the chosen ones of the holiness, I still don't know what does that mean but I know I can do impossible possible through the power of Father, Sara was just looking at him, John continued saying, I am half Angel too but have no wings, Sara didn't move at all, John said: this is the thing that I have been keeping hidden from you, I just came to know about it in . . . Sara said: are there some hidden cameras in here? Are you making fun of me? Is it some Hollywood scene? Okay come out guys!, John couldn't believe of what he was hearing, he said: Sara please! there is no time to joke, let me show it to you again, and he started concentrating but he couldn't as so many thoughts were going around in his mind, and Sara laughed, she said: enough Mr. Seven you got me, good one, tell them to go out of my home now, I don't like people seeing my private things, John felt disappointed but didn't Loose his hope, he said: Sara leave everything just lets go to the shop, so Sara put the readymade meal in the fridge, and said: lets go.

Together they went to the nearest shop where they thought they could get some Chocó kokoes, so after searching for a while they found a place, named Come and Get Kokoey* (the shop looked like a bar of chocolate from outside, it looked very chic),

John and Sara entered into the place and sat on the chairs which looked like pieces of chocolates. Johns stomach made a loud noise which made people around him to start looking at him, John looked at everyone and said: good morning good people, I haven't eaten anything yet so forgive the sounds my stomach makes, but people didn't even give him a simple smile, just like they had no feelings or any interest in him, John looked at Sara and said: slowly, people are growing colder every year, after awhile a waiter came forward, he looked like a long chocolate shake glass on which there was some cream, the costume looked nice but the waiter looked very strange, the waiter had wrinkled eyes, looked very weak, and look intolerable, as usual Sara was looking at the menu and wasn't finding anything, John slowly said: we came here to drink Chocó koko remember, Sara looked at him and said: of course, and looked at the waiter, then said: two large Chocó koko please!, the waiter (uninterestingly) wrote down the order and went towards the kitchen.

John started looking around as usual, he looked at the table that they were sitting around it, the strawberry shape chairs, the artificial bananas and the other fruits which were hanging around the place, the floor which looked like it was made from cream, while looking he noticed there was statue of God.SED at one of the corners of the shop, John got suspicious and suddenly an Earth Quake shook the land, John immediately jumped on the table and covered Sara`s head, the Earth Quake wasn't powerful but was enough to shake everything, after it was over, Sara looked at John and Said: wow! I did make a right choice of becoming your Future wife, you do love me so much!, John smiled and said: you haven't seen anything yet my lady, then he sat on the chair, the waitresses and the waiters told to the people in the shop that due to developments at the Temples building, the land was shaken so everybody calmed down, but John felt there was nothing right with that unusual Earth Quake but he didn't pay attention to that and started looking around again, he looked at the people in the shop again, he felt as everything was normal and okay but very soon he realised nothing was right in there, a man was drinking from his nose, a woman was pasting chocolate cake on her children faces and then was licking them, an old man was biting the walls and the rest of the people were involved in other strange things, while looking he heard some unusual foot stepping way, he turned around and saw a tall woman who was wearing a very long black winter coat was going through the rest rooms, while looking at her Sara pushed him a bit and said: John I am going to the rest room, do you wanna come with me? John was so involved looking at the woman that he didn't even answer Saras question, Sara made some face and slowly said: sometimes he is active and horny and sometimes totally a gay and went towards the restrooms, after few seconds John stood up and he too went towards the restroom by following the strange woman, the woman didn't go to the ladies room and instead went to the Gents room which made John very suspicious. He stopped until the woman entered the restroom and then he slowly went near the door and opened it quietly, the woman removed her coat, she was neither a man nor a woman, she was a large Demon, the Demon started peeing on the wall and made some strange sounds, John slowly entered into the place and locked the door behind himself, and moved closer to the Demon, the Demon looked like an Ogre, the Ogres eyes were closed but suddenly he turned around and looked straight in Johns eyes, then said: in a very broken human language, I have been expecting you since the moment you came in the shop!, John was very scared but he was controlling his fear as he knew he had some powers to stand against Evil creatures, John looked at him in a very serious way and said: why have you come here!, the Ogre bowed down and said: I came here to serve you my lord, John was shocked, he said: lord? What are you talking about? The Ogre looked at him and said; very soon you will lead the army of Master Darkness and will win the battle against the light!, John looked very confused, he said: no I will not!, I will fight against Darkness to win the battle for my Father! The Ogre ran to him picked him up with his left hand and threw him into the toilets and said: so you will die now; John: was smacked into the toilets and broke everything. The pipes broke as well and the water had boosted out, the Ogre said: I came to protect you but if you are not on our side then you will not survive, John turned around and rolled a bit on the floor and hardly stood up, he then closed his eyes and concentrated. The layer of energy started appearing around him, then he opened his eyes and said: you came at the wrong time and a very wrong place, he then ran towards the Oger punched him in the face, the power of the punch was so high that the Oger was thrown into the wall and broke it, John then ran to the oger faster than before but Oger stood up before John had reached to him and kicked John into the stomach but John controlled himself and wasn't thrown away and they started fighting, he punched and then ogre, people who wanted to come to the rest room were standing behind the door and all were shocked by the noises they were hearing, meanwhile John punched the Ogre in his jaw and then shouted and said: by the power of my father I command you to be destroyed, and energy wave was blown from John, the wave terminated the Ogre and also destroyed the whole bathroom which made its wall to collapse, when John looked around he saw the time was moving very slowly for him, the bricks were flouting in the air, the water was slowly spreading everywhere, even the blood which was coming from his face and mouth was falling slowly, he looked at the people who were standing behind the broken walls, he then quickly concentrated and said: by the power of my father I heal my wounds, when he opened his eyes he was all healed up, so before the time reached to its normal movement he ran out of the restroom and sat where he was sitting before, and very shortly the time started moving normally, all the people in the shop screamed and rushed towards the bathroom, Sara came out of the rest room and ran to John, she said: what happened? John replied: I guess someone's bottom was blown away and laughed, Sara said: do you feel really hungry? John said: we better get the heck out of here, Sara nodded and they went outside the shop, John was amazed by seeing large number of P.SED and Sky eyes around the place, so he just put his head down and crossed from the place. As quick as he could because John knew that the Sky eyes were very accurate in what they were searching for, and they would have found out everything about the incidents within a very short period of time.

After walking for a while; Sara asked: why these days passed like that huh? John looked at her and said: God knows what will happen next, he then said: hey do you wanna go visit uncle number 6? She looked at him in a confusing way and said: uncle number 6? I thought he had passed away, some years ago?, John looked down and said: no he didn't he just closed the shop because no one wanted to be classic anymore and see classics anymore, Sara asked: so what are we waiting for? John smiled and said: lets go then. They then moved towards the uncle number 6 shop. While walking, a group of P.SED members entered into the street and announced that the weather was going to get cold within two hours and snow would fall sooner than that, so people rushed to their houses to get some warm cloths and the stuff that they would need, John looked at himself and Sara and said: we gotta get some cloths, so they went to a very fancy cloths shop and bought, winter Booths, long Coats, Gloves, winter Hats and all the other items that they needed, and continued moving towards the shop.

After awhile of walking they reached to the place, it was a very old building, the walls had crack on them, the roof was broken, the paint of the wall was removed in most of its place, the windows were sealed by concrete, the door of the building was made by Iron and was rusted, it looked very old and short as well, by looking at the building anyone would notice that there couldn't be the present of any activities in it, but John moved towards the door, he looked around so he could feel secure and then he knocked the door 6 times slowly, and stood back, a very strong voice was heard, a man said: why? John while hugging Sara said: because God loves us and wants us to go to Heaven, the door was opened immediately, a hairy hand came out and pulled Sara and John inside.

A very old and short man was standing inside, he had no hairs, he had a pale face and his back was bent, he was wearing a very old gray jacket and a very old black pant as well as shoes, when he saw John and Sara he hugged them and said: we have been waiting for you for a long time, we missed your presence in here, Sara still couldn't believe that she was standing inside the shop as it was almost 4 years since the last time she has been there and she was very thrilled to see Alex(the old man), Alex helped them to remove their jackets and said: it is almost impossible to adjust with this different weather in a very short time, he took a deep breath and said: it will change, everything will go back to normal, and then opened the basements door for them, but before they went down John looked at Alex and said: by the way how have you guys been? Alex while relocating his artificial teeth said: ahh! you know us, we are the same old men and women, and do party every day and laughed, John laughed too and said: I wish everyone had such powerful Spirit like the one you guys have and then along with Sara went downstairs.

The basement looked like a big dancing stage, and was decorated by cowboy's items; it looked like a bar at Texas. The people in the basement were all Cowboys and Farmers, the place was made by wood and was shining very much, at the middle of the floor a country singer was singing a very beautiful song and the rest of the people were laughing, dancing, singing and having fun, Sara looked at John and said: why haven't you told me that this place was still active? John replied: because the last time you punched a girl in the face just because she had told you a strict British girl!, so I thought you would keep punching everyone if I would bring you here, Sara smiled and said: well you did right but I am a better person now so I won't punch anyone anymore, while they were talking, uncle number 6 saw them and shouted, he said: yiiihahaha look who`s here? My son and my beautiful daughter, the place became completely silent and everyone turned and looked at John and Sara, John and Sara almost shocked and got a bit shy, then John raised his hand up and said: hi guys, it's very cool to see you all again, uncle number 6 jumped from a chair and picked John up and said: my boy is back, John while being squeezed said: yes! yes! indeed he is back, and the crowd laughed and one by one came to greet them, after everyone had greeted them. John and Sara went with uncle number 6 into his office, the office was a very simple one, there were many Cowboy hats on the walls, many pictures from Texas, Farmers and his wife around the place too, John and Sara sat on the chair, uncle number 6 stood near the door and said: I am gonna get you some Hot Number 6 Chocolate glasses and will be right back and he shut the door.

Sara held Johns hand and said: this place looks beautiful, there is life in here, people have feelings in here, up there looks like a Machine World with a lot of Robots who have no work to do except having Sex!, John laughed and said: it's true, world has been changed, but who can stop it, this life is what most of them want, so be cool!.

Then he looked at the picture of uncle number 6 which was on the table, he was a young man when he took that photo, he was holding his wife(Joy) hand and they were laughing, they looked so peaceful, so happy, John closed his eyes and thought about uncle number 6 and his wife.

Uncle number 6 was an old man who went to Canada from Austin Texas many years ago with his wife Joy, his real name was Jamie, he was around 180cm tall, having short hair at all times, blue eyes, and had a bit of extra weight, he was the best hot chocolate maker in the city, he had his own shop and house, he was famous as uncle number 6 because it was his best flavour Hot Chocolate glass, he had numbers for his different flavours, but because his 6th flavour was the best people used to call him uncle number 6, he didn't have any kids, some said he couldn't some, said he didn't want to, some said other things but no one really knew what was the reason behind it, he was a very kind and respectable man, he believed in God more than he believed in anything, he used to read the Holy Book with John whenever he used to go to his house and he had a very nice wife as well. Joy was around 154cm tall, had short brown hair, blue eyes, fair, and had normal body size, she loved children very much as she didn't have children, she used to adore John and Sara at all time, but unfortunately she passed away some years ago because of Cancer, she had lung Cancer, doctors told her it was because of the Pollution in the air but who could have change her future, doctors gave her the option to fight against the Cancer but she didn't want to, she believed that if her time was coming she had to let it come so she past away sooner that anyone would expect, she loved Jamie very much, since she died, Jamie closed the shop, as he got depressed but he reopened it downstairs for those who believed in the true God, to enjoy, cheer and also to create a faithful God loving family.

While John was thinking Jamie came inside the room, he was holding a very large tray on which there were two large glasses of Hot Chocolate, he then put the glasses in front of them and while smiling he sat on his leather chair. He looked at John and Sara and said: I really missed you guys, well I missed you much more my beloved daughter, why have you stopped coming in here?, Sara looked at John, then said; because somebody thought I would hit someone in the face again, John made some faces and said: oh come on give me a break! What would anyone do huh? Then he laughed and drank some Hot Chocolate and said: ohhh ya! Feels just like Heaven, how long have I not been in here? Jamie said: 1 year, 6 days, and many hours, John drank some more Hot Chocolate and said: I love you for your sharp memory uncle and laughed. Jamie then looked at Sara and said: how have you been my dear? Sara while drinking said: pretty good, had some issues with John lately but you know him, everyday he does something that makes me more in love with him, Jamie smiled and said: this is called love!, this is what God has given us which makes us different, this is what this life is all about, look at me its been long time since the last time I kissed your aunt and had her but I am still loving her and never cheated on her till the present moment.

John drank some more Hot Chocolate and said: I will walk on your footsteps uncle, he then held Sara's` hand and said: I won't let this Jewel to be taken from me, Sara just smiled and a bit shied.

Jemmy looked at John in a very serious way and said: the Oracle is here with us today. John shocked and spread some Hot chocolate out of his mouth. Sara looked at them doubtfully and asked: what is Oracle? Jamie looked at her and said: she is a blind old lady who has come back from Hell; she has no eyes but sees everything, she remembers everything and knows everything about the future Sara laughed said: oh you are kidding right? Jamie looked at her very seriously and said: this life is not a joke and the things she says are not too, then Sara (wondering) said: then like, what do we have to do now? Like do we need to go to see her or . . . John nodded his head and said: we indeed need to go and see her, so they stood up and all went to the main hall.

Jamie went to another room and then came out, took the microphone and said: she is ready to speak, so all the people sat on the chairs around and kept silent, Jamie went in the room and came out while holding the Oracles hand. The Oracle looked very old, she had white long hair, very old skin, and was very weak, she was also wearing a very old purple color dress, and Jamie helped her to sit on a chair and then switched all the lights except the one which was at the top of the place where Oracle was sitting. The Oracle thanked him and started speaking by a very weak voice.

She told them about her life story, she said she was a very bad and a trouble maker child, she used to live in a large family in which there were 8 other children, she said her parents couldn't handle any one of them, so she almost grew up by her own, she said that she was a very Horny girl since her childhood, she used to go to her brothers and ask them to show their Penises to her, she said she losed her virginity when she was 12 years old, these words made John very angry, she said she got involved into Drugs, Drinking, Smocking and Prostitution, she never cared about anything around her except her own stomach, she put her head down and said: I even cut many people by a sharp blade as I need Drugs and they didn't give it to me, she then smiled and said: I finally got saved by a very kind gentleman who she didn't want to say his name, she said she started believing in God and doing good things to forget about her past, she cleaned the Drugs from her body system by going through some painful treatments, she started exercising and also started studying again, she said life started becoming very good to her, she made a lot of good friends, believed in God and read the Holy Book at all time, she went into church every single day as she wanted to get more close to God, she said her life was changed after believing in him, the people in who were sitting cheered for her, and said loudly Praise the lord most high!, but the Oracle nodded her head and said: let me tell you the rest of the story, so everyone kept quite again, she said: even though my life was changed, even though I had no problems at all and I used to go to Church and read the Holy Book at all time, I still had not really surrendered myself into his hands, I used to believe in him but deep down there in my heart I was a faithless girl. I just simply couldn't follow the heavenly rules, I knew i was suppose to stand against my passion and desires but I simply couldn't, I fell in love with the Pastor who led my eyes opened, I told her that I loved him but he had made an oath with God that he would never marry, he was the most incredible man I had ever seen, when I would see him, I would think of nothing except making love to him, the crowd laughed out loud but John looked very angry, she then said: I couldn't control myself, I called him to come to my home and visit me, when he came I locked the door and striped off, some boys whistled in the hall, John got very angry and realised that his Holy Sign had started glowing so he controlled his anger, the Oracle said: he closed his eyes and said: what are you doing dear? Have you forgotten about the rules? I ran to him and started kissing him on the face and everywhere that I could, but he pushed me back and said: you still have Evil Spirit in you, God has given us this gift to make love but he has also given us the power to stop the temptation, I didn't know what to do I just wanted him to hold me, touch me, kiss me, I could do anything for him, he was disappointed in me he gently just raised his hand and said: let me pray for you, I just wanted to feel him so I gave my hand to him, and he prayed, she smiled and said: I remember all the words he said: (Father thank you once again for letting us have control over our desires and wills, Father I want to give . . . (the Oracle didn't say her name), into thy hand as you are the true owner of our souls, I want you to bless her and her soul so that this temptation be taken from her heart and she starts becoming a better servant for you, Oracle smiled and said: I was so horny in that moment that I didn't realise what he meant, he prayed and prayed and then while his eyes were closed, he slowly said: I know that you are a very well woman but don't let Evil to enter into your body again, I couldn't control myself I went to kiss his lips but he shouted and said: please control yourself, for I have no intention to be with you at all, the words slammed a door in my head, I became very angry and threw him out of my house and never went back to see him again and never continued practicing the faith and went back to the same old days, I started Prostituting, Drinking, Smoking and a lot of other worse things and once when I was very drunk I fell from a balcony of a house of a Pimp while I was screaming for help I remembered his face, I wanted to see him one more time to say that I was sorry but it was too late, I was smacked into the ground and (sorrowfully) said: died, people in the shop were really shocked and also felt really sorrowful for her.

She said: when I opened my eyes I was in the place called . . . John slowly said: Nowhere land but it was Hell for me, a man raised his voice and said: I am sorry to say this but you did deserve that didn't you? She nodded her head and said: indeed I deserved it, she then said: that place was worse than what we have heard, read in stories or have seen in movies, in there you hear nothing except the souls who are crying out loud, being attacked by Demons, and screams oh! It is a very horrible place; I wonder how the Real Hell will look like!? She then continued saying: the entire place was covered by Darkness, the only light was coming from the flames of fire and the burning ground, I have been there for along time as the time moves very slow in there. We souls were being tortured, attacked, and burnt by the Evil powers around us, there was no place to escape, we were shouting out loud for help but there was no one to help us in there, a woman raised her voice up and said: then how did you get out of there? The Oracle said: i made a deal, I prayed while I was burning and I told to God that I was sorry for the sins that I had done, I still have no idea why father had forgave me, but now I realise that he wanted me to do good by coming back to Earth, even though I have no heart beats and flesh but still I am alive, I told to God that I would do anything to make him proud if he would give me a chance, and as he is the loving and caring Father he did grant me this opportunity and I am very glad of it and praise him more than ever and suddenly she said: how is it possible! People looked at her very doubtfully and confusingly and asked her what was wrong? The Oracle raised her finger up towards John and said: I cannot believe he is here and he is among us, I finally found him after all these years of searching, a boy who thought she was pointing at him said: are you talking about me Ma'am? She said: him John the Seventh, John couldn't believe of what he was hearing, even Sara couldn't believe about the things happening around them, the Oracle said: come! come my lord, this is Gods mercy to have you in here, John looked at her (very shocked and confused) and moved towards her, he stood beside her and said: Ma'am I am . . . the Oracle said: your glory is much more than I thought, look at your flesh you have such powerful blessed blood, John didn't really like the words she was saying as he was really suspect full towards her, so he concentrate and started looking at the true image of her, he saw a very weak soul was standing and her eyes were covered by two large hands, which looked like the hands of a bat, the Oracle said: you are about to change the whole world very soon, John (very shocked): what? Almost everyone in the room said the same words, Sara came forward and said louder what? The Oracle said: all the creatures in Heaven and Hell know about you as you are the decision maker and the future changer, John couldn't say anything he didn't know what to say? She said: the decisions you make will change our lives, even though I have the blessings of foretelling the future, can`t tell yours, but I can see the power rushing through your body, it is beautiful, bless me by Lords power let me see again, John was totally shocked, there was a very bitter cold silence in the room, John closed his eyes, put his hand on the Oracles eyes and said: by the power of my Father I command these Evil hands to be separated from your eyes and you see again, his hand started glowing and the Oracle started seeing again, people in the place losed their control, they saw happening Miracle in front of their eyes, Sara didn't look very happy but she smiled, the Oracle hugged John and said: you will make a difference in this world, John replied: I will not, Father will, I will just do my best to make him proud, John then looked at the rest and said: good people, I believe the end is coming sooner than we thought, meanwhile he was speaking, a group of P.SED members who had taken all the information regarding John and Saras lives from Michelle had searched for them and reached to the building, one of them who looked like he was the leader, smelled the door and said: they are here and they started breaking the door and enter inside, everyone in the basement heard the noises and scared, the Oracle looked at John and said: they have come to take you John, run and go far from here before it is too late, John said: we may loose our lives in this world but we will have it back in the next, the Oracle said: but you will never die as you are not a human, you are the blessed one the future changer, Jamie looked around and said: my brothers, sisters and children, this is the time to show our true faith for Father, he then looked at John and said: get the Hell out of here my boy, I will see you in Heaven one day, then he opened a secret door which would lead them to the other side of the building and said: go my children go!, John held Saras hand and rushed towards the door, while going the Oracle said: fight for him not your Love. After they went out, Jamie looked at the rest and asked: who will stay and fight against the Evil? And who will go away from here as the door is yet open!?

No one moved a bit, a Cowboy was putting bullets in his Shot Gun, he said: let us show these sons of bitches, what we Cowboys can really do, and the rest of the people shouted out loud and said: praise the lord highest!, and then Jamie shut the door and locked it.

The New Heaven & the New Earth . . . .

A very young female Angel asked a question from John: she said: weren't you scared? John smiled and replied: who wouldn't be scared in that moment

Story time . . .

John and Sara were climbing the stairs as fast as they could; John wasn't thinking about things, he had one thought that was to save Sara. Climbing those stairs was the toughest thing that John had ever done in his life, he looked at Sara, her tears were falling, she was very afraid, John got angry, he knew from then onwards everything would be different, he knew they were in trouble and this time it was very big one, while they were going up, John prayed in his heart he said: Father save us from Evil, be with us in this difficult time and protect us, he heard the sound of screams and Gun shots, he knew people in the shop were in trouble but couldn't go back and help them, after climbing up for awhile, they reached to a closed door which separated the basement from the street behind it, John hit himself into it and broke it as it was very old.

Sara looked at John and while her tears were falling asked: what now John? What now? Am I dreaming? What is this life all about? John hugged her and said: everything will be alright!, they both started feeling cold as, outside was snowing, Sara started shivering as she was wearing a simple sweater only, John removed his sweater and made her to wear it, he wasn't feeling cold that much as he was controlling his power so he was feeling warm inside his body.

A group of P.SED members were walking on the street and were announcing that a couple name John Seven and Sara Thomson are recognised as Criminals and if they were seen must have been immediately informed!, Sara hugged John tight and said: what now what now John, I am very scared!, John said: easy! Easy!, God is with us, don't worry, but inside he himself didn't know what to do? Where could he go? He thought of going back home but he had to cross from middle of the streets which would let people to recognise them and he knew if they would stay there, very soon they would get arrested, he closed his eyes and prayed again, Father show me the way, please help us, and felt an unusual warmness around his Holy sign, he looked at it and saw it was shining, Sara looked up and saw the Sign, then said: when did you get that? You tell me not to get Tattoo and you have got one already? John said: does it look like a Tattoo to you?, this is . . . he heard some P.SED members were talking together and realised that they were moving towards the place John and Sara were standing but before he thought of doing something, the P.SED members stood right at the beginning of the street and while smiling moved towards them, Sara started crying she said: I am scared John do something please! Please!.

John held her hand tight and said: no matter what happens next don't come out of here (he pointed towards the stairs which they climbed up) Sara tried not to leave him but John pushed her and then closed the old broken door, he looked at the P.SED members who were now standing very close to him, he concentrate and started seeing their true images, all of them were wild Demons, he said today we will have fun pieces of shit!, the Demons roared at him, and suddenly some Sky eyes members landed in front of them by their flying vehicle, the P.SED members put their head down and stepped back.

The Sky eyes members moved forward, John hasn't seen such Evil Beast that close ever before, one of the Beasts roared at him and in broken human language said: you have killed one of us back in the Restaurant which proved that you are not one of us even though you will lead us in future . . . John shouted and said; Ah! shut up! you Evil creature, I will never lead you and your Evil Masters army, he then concentrated and the energy layers started appearing around him, the Beast smiled and said: so be it, and they both attacked each other, but this time John wasn't feeling the pain very much, it was like his body had turned into Metal, they fought and fought, when the P.SED members saw that John wasn't getting defeated they moved in the fight as well, and because they were many they succeed in defeating John and they threw him towards the building in front of them, John was smacked into the wall, the wall was broken and he went inside the building, the Evil members looked at each other and in Evil language said: he wants to lead us in future and laughed, then the Beast said: look! Look at there! Pointing towards Sara, Sara was crying and was very afraid, he said: let's get her and take her to the Temple, but the ground shook, one of the Demons said: what was that?, they turned around and looked at the building where John was smacked into it, and suddenly a huge explosion happened, the whole place was covered by light, the building where John was smack into was blown away, he was lucky that no one lived there as it was very old, the time started moving slowly, the Beasts and Demons looked at John and saw an Angel standing, he was glowing so much that the Beasts and Demons couldn't look at him continuously, the energy layers around John were very brighter, Johns eyes were closed, he opened them and ran with a very fast speed towards the Evil creatures, and said; by the power of my Father I will terminate you all and blew a very powerful energy wave, the windows of all the building broke and fell down all the buildings had got large cracks, the Beasts and Demons were terminated, even the ground had got a large crack on it, Johns eyes were closed and when he opened he was hugging Sara, before the explosion terminate everything, he rushed to Sara and covered her as he was not getting harmed by the waves.

Sara opened her eyes and screamed, as John was glowing very much and his eyes were covered by a very bright light, John smiled and said: what happened, my deepest love? Sara said: John you are really an Angel!, I ammm I just don't know what to say, its like being in a Hollywood movie, John smiled and said: they make movies from the true stories that`s why you think like this, then his brightness disappeared, John could now feel everything stronger, he could hear better, smell better, he could see better. So he heard more Evil members were moving towards them, so he looked at Sara and said: we need to get out of here now, they climbed the stairs again and looked around, John saw some cloths of Evil members were on the snow full ground and also their flying vehicles looked useable yet, so John told to Sara to wear the Beasts cloths so they could not be recognised. So they looked at the cloths which they could wear and even though they didn't want to wear them, but they did, while John was wearing the cloth, he looked at Sara, she was shivering but she removed all her cloths to get fit into those tight cloths, so he started dreaming and singing love songs in his mind, Sara pulled a zip up and turned and said: hey!!! John got himself together and said: we must marry somehow, my blood is boiling for you, she stepped forward and pulled up John's cloth's zip and said: you get naughty sometimes and sometimes very soft, is it because you are an Angel? John kissed her nose then said: it could be and laughed, then looked at the flying vehicles, and said: how are we going to fly them up? Sara replied: we will not fly with those creepy things, I am afraid of heights, but John held her hand and sat on the vehicle. The vehicle had no wheels, no buttons, nothing, there was just two hand places where the Sky eyes used to put their hands in, John wanted to put his hands inside the places but he remembered that the machines were flying Demons themselves so he could get hurt or into trouble, so he looked at the vehicle and said: by the power of my Father I command you to be blessed and work for good, the color of the vehicle changed from black into white, John looked at the vehicle with his blessed power and saw the Demon was gone, so he put his hands inside the hand places and the vehicle immediately got separated from the land, John and Sara losed their balances but after a short time got it back, Sara while hugging John tightly said: I told you I am afraid of the heights and more over have you noticed that these tiny cloths make you feel warmer than the large ones we were wearing? John while controlling the balance said: I just did, and heard someone shouting behind them, he turned around and saw Many P.SED members and the Sky eyes members were running through them, John control the balance and said: hold on tight! and they flew up, Sara screamed and said: I hate heights and while flying they went far and far, several Sky eyes too flew behind them and followed them.

While flying, Sara turned around and screamed again, she said; John look!, John turned around and saw many Sky eyes members were flying behind them and they all looked very angry, one of them pointed his finger towards John and released an Energy Bomb*(the very concentrated energy which acts like a hand Grenade)towards them, the energy bomb hit the bottom of the vehicle and destructed it badly, the vehicle started losing its balance, Sara was just screaming in that moment and was shouting for help. John looked at her and said: give me your hands, Sara while screaming said: what are you crazy? John removed his hands out of the hand places, which made the vehicle to get switched off and very quickly put Saras hands inside of them, he then stood up and while the vehicle was going down very fast, he moved and stood behind Sara and shout: Sara control the vehicle I gotta jump to the Sky eyes and beat them and then get one of their vehicles!, Sara screamed again and said: how on Earth can I . . . . . and John jumped, while jumping he concentrated so the time started moving slower for him, he reached himself to one of the Sky eyes members (the time went back to normal), and then he shouted and said: by the power of my

Father . . . suddenly he heard a voice, it looked like it was coming out from the sky, the voice told him: I am the leader of all Angels, Gabriel, you may not need to repeat the words that you say as Father has blessed you and you can use your powers without using his glorious name continuously, and then the voice was gone, John smiled and said: life has never been better than this, so while fighting with one of the Sky eyes, he remembered the way he had attacked, a few minutes ago, so he raised his hand up and said: I call this the Light Bomb, he then released an energy wave through one of the Sky eyes and terminated him instantly, he then smiled and said: it is show time ladies and Gentlemen and started jumping from one vehicle to the others, while he was punching and releasing the Light bombs, he was singing too, he was singing everybody wants kung fu fighting, and he was punching, blocking, kicking the Sky eyes members again and again, but one of the Sky eyes members punched him with a supernatural power that made his mouth to bleed out, he cleaned the blood and said; (angrily) and now is the Collaborating time, and released a bigger Light bomb throw the Sky eyes members, and started terminating them faster and faster, he was in fact so fast that he could see his own Light bombs moving throw the Evil members, so within a short time, he terminated all the Evil members, got one of their vehicles and flew to Sara, Sara was still screaming, John pulled her from the vehicle she was sitting on, into the vehicle he was sitting on it, and then said: calm down sweetie I am right here, Sara shouted and said: why some unusual lights keep coming out of your eyes? John laughed and said: good question but I have no answer, as their fortune they crossed just from the top of Johns house and both were very shocked by what they just saw, Johns house was collapsed, it looked like it had gotten on fire, many people and P.SED members were standing around the house, Sara started crying, John became angry and said: we gotta go to the Temple and finish the business, so he accelerate more and they both moved towards the Old Caspian Sea.

The Temple of God.SED . . .

A Sky eyes member rushed inside the Temple, kneeled and said: (in Evil language): Master, forgive me for interrupting your precious work but this is an emergency, God.SED was laying on a very large bed which was made by Gold and Diamonds and was mating with several women, and kissing them opened his eyes, pushed the women away, stood on the bed while he was nude and loudly ordered everyone to go out immediately, all the workers left the room and closed the door behind them.

God.SED shouted and said: you can't even handle some powerless humans, the rain of fire started falling on peoples bodies from outside the Temple, which made everyone and everything to get burnt and made the State of Emergency condition for people,

God.SED shouted: and in Evil language said: the time has come, a dark mist covered on all over his body and he transformed into the Monsters that John had seen on the T.V, the Sky eyes member also transformed, Evil(Bigger Monster) looked at the Sky eyes member and said(in Evil language): we have not come on Earth to get failed because of some powerless creatures, he then raised his left finger up, the Sky eyes member was cut into half immediately and fell on the floor and his black and unholy blood was spread everywhere, and then two giant hands of fire came out of the floor and took the dead body of the Sky eyes member inside the Earth, (the hands looked like the hands of humans but with long and black nails, the hand were to burning like the flames of fire), he then called all the workers of the Temple to enter inside the room that he was in, and the workers entered, by seeing him changed they all had also changed into their true images. He then asked them all about John; one of the Demons came forward and in Evil language said: Master he is the one we were searching for, he is the Chosen one, Evil smiled, looking at Devil (Small Monster) said: impressive!, and slowly started moving side to side, then he said: you miserable weak creatures will not be able to defeat him as per the prophecy but my Fire-eyes*(they were giant Demons, they were immortal against the Holy powers, they were made as soldier to fight in the battle, they were originally made from human blood which was mixed with the Evil and Devils bloods and were result of mating with humans, they did not have eyes as fire flames were coming out of them, they physically looked like a long bat in red color, but did not have wings or tail) are strong enough to destroy him, Devil yawned and said: so what are we waiting for huh? And he clapped, large number of Fire-eyes entered into the place and stood in the proper lines, all the other creature put their heads down and stood back.

The leader of the Fire-eyes came forward and kneeled, he then said: Master how can we be at your service?, Evil disappeared and reappeared in front of him and touched his head, the leader looked up and turned towards the Fire-eyes and roared out loud, and they all disappeared.

Evil smiled and said: my anger made me forget about the people, who are dying outside and burning and laughed Evilly, then said: let us go out and make a better day for them as very soon they will become our Slaves, all the creatures started laughing and cheering for him. And then he looked at the Evil and they recombined together and transformed into their human forms.

People were screaming and crying outside and all around the world, everything was under fire and burning, many places were destroyed, many people died, because before the rain of fire snow had covered the land, the water level had gone very high abnormally which had caused into the creation of Floods, Tsunamis and many other Natural Disasters, so the world looked like a big State of Emergency.

Many people had gathered together and were protesting in front of the Temple and were being pushed back by P.SED members, suddenly a very long Rainbow appeared in the Sky, which was seen by all the people around the world.

Suddenly the land around the Temple shook and God.SED, standing on his Marble made Pillar came out of the center of the Temple and moved high and higher, he then sat on his Gold made chair and loudly said: my children why are you forsaking me? Please calm down; there is an explanation behind the sudden Omen.

People were still shouting and protesting, some old people were giving slogans and had drawn a cross on God.SED picture, God.SED started looking very angry, he shouted and stroke some of the people and terminated them, a very cold and bitter silence covered the whole place, God.SED shouted and said: enough is enough you miserable creatures, and several lightening stroke the land, he then said: you have everything that you desire and you still forsake me?

What I have to do to make you controlled, do you need me to give an end to this beautiful place? While he was speaking a small girl moved forward, she was dressed in Ancient Roman Fashion, she had short blond hair, very fair and was playing with her Doll, she then screamed and said: shut up! you bad God, I hate you, God.SED turned red, several lightnings stroke the land, then put his hands beside each other from side and then slowly separated them, the child was tore off from the middle of her legs and catch on fire, her parents cried out loud and tried to save her but they couldn't, people scared to Death, God.SED then loudly said: I count her Death as my Peacemaking Offering with you faithless creatures.

People around the place where speechless, they were all scared to Death and were really confused too, God.SED raised his voice out loud and said: how dare any one of you dare to say such words against me!, and he stroke some more people and terminated them, he said: it is true, no power can control you all, and several lightnings stroke the land, he stretched his head to sides and said: (very angry) I feel the time is right and has come to finish the unfinished business that I came for, people perished, they started crying and begging him to forgive them, some people sacrificed several different Animals for his sake, many parents brought their virgin girls forward pushed them in front of the P.SED members and fell on the ground saying please forgive us!, but meanwhile a group of true God believers came forward and protested against him, they said: what type of a God you are that you need us suffer for your sake huh? A Muslim man who looked very Afghani, came forward and said; Curse be on you forever!, a Christian came forward and said: the Lord is with us he will give an end to this Evil work of yours, several other people from different religions stepped forward and holding hands said: we will fight for the true God as we had fought for all these years, God bless us all and free us from you Evil creatures, several P.SED members attacked them and started battling with them. People had losed their control, some were screaming, some were crying, some were fighting against the P.SED members and also among themselves, some even were kissing as they thought they would get stroke by the God.SED.

God.SED looked at them for a while, and slowly a very large and dark cloud appeared in the Sky, he looked much more reddish than before, he closed his fingers and several Lightnings stroke the ground, he then waved his hand a bit and a very speedy wind blew towards the people, he then waved his hands up and down and an Earth Quake shook the land, people scared very much, some of them left everything and fell on the ground and started worshiping him. God.SED looked at people for a bit more time and then shouted very loud, he then said: you have made my heart harden for you and you will now pay the price, he raised his left hand up towards a group of people who were protesting against him and said: enjoy your painful and harsh Death the people started burning, but were not dying, they were continuously burning and screaming, by seeing such Omen all the people fell on the ground and started begging P.SED to forgive them.

God.SED smiled and in his mind said: bow to me for now, soon you will bow to me forever and I will make you all my Slaves, he then raised his voice up and said: do you want them to be saved from the flames? People crying replied: yes! please help them, God.SED looked at the clouds and a very heavy rain started falling, he then clapped and the weather changed into a very Sunny and normal day, just like no rain and snow had fallen before, he then looked at the burning people and the fires disappeared and even they had received their healthiness back which made them to lose their faith in the real God and start worshiping him.

God.SED sat on his chair and very calmly said: look my beloved children, I have given you, your senses as I have them all, so sometimes when you behave improper, my heart gets harden, so I punish you but I am the God of love, and love you all, people started smiling, he said: the things I do is my business and you shall not put me under questions as I am your God, he then stood up and said: for all who are still not believing in me, I have a clear message, I am the Beginning and the End of this world, and he pointed his finger into an area in front of the Temple, and the area shook a bit, and separated from sides, then flames of fire burst out of the large crack, people started worshiping him louder by saying you are the owner of all Heat and Fires, he then looked at the Sky above him, a large cloud appeared and started twisting into itself and from the middle of it a large river of water came out and stroke the burning fire and mixed with it, people shouted: louder and said: you are the owner of Waters he then closed his eyes and a very power full wind was blown into the crowd and started rotating around the mixture of Water and Fire and gave the mixer a higher speed, by seeing such power many perished, God.SED opened his eyes and opened his hands, and then closed them, the Sand, Dust and some parts of Soil were taken from the ground and had been mixed into the mixture, people started singing, dancing and rejoicing, as they never had seen such power and such supernatural activities ever before, they shouted out loud and praised him as their powerful God.

Meanwhile John and Sara were still on the vehicle and could see the Temple and the large crowd around it, they couldn't believe of what they were looking at, the Temple looked like a large worshiping point and all the people were bowing towards it, Sara while hugging John very tightly said: never leave me alone John!, John turned his face around and said: what do you mean by that? Without you I am nothing!, I love you more than anything else on this Earth!, Sara laid her head on his back and said: but you don't love me more than God do you?, John replied: Sara that's a different love, he is our creator, he is the one who every one must love first, as he is the truth and the owner of our souls but I love you so much, more than anything that you can imagine, Sara said: will you stay with me till the End of time? John said: why till then?, I will stay and be with you forever, Sara said: I need you John! Please don't leave me and her tears fell down, John said: (very gently) are you thinking about the words that the Oracle said? Oh come on Sara!, she came from Hell what can she really know about everything?, Sara replied saying: but she was right you are an Angel and I am nothing, John said: who cares what I am or what you are as long as I love you and you love me, Sara cried louder and said: I feel scared John please don't leave me!, Johns heart was beating very fast while listening to what she was telling him, he turned around his face again, looked at her and said: I will never leave you Sara, no matter what happens I will stay with you, and while he was talking he slowly headed down, and landed between two large buildings which looked like two pieces of Bananas, they then got off from the vehicle, and stood on the street.

Sara hugged John again and said: promise me that you will not leave me alone, John said: hey! Hey! Now stop saying that!, why are you thinking like this and he was thrown into the wall, Sara screamed out loud and looked around, many Fire-eyes were standing very close to them, the leader of them came forward removed John from the wall he had crashed in and punched him through the Evil members, the Fire-eyes members started beating him as much as they could and because John wasn't able to concentrate, he had started bleeding so much and was hurt very badly, while he was getting beaten, one of the female Fire-eyes moved and grabbed Sara's hands from behind and started licking her, in that time Sara was not only screaming for help but also screaming as she was afraid of the face of the Fire-eyes member, while the Fire-eyes member was licking Sara, she grabbed her cloth's zip and slowly started opening it which would make Sara to get naked, but before she opened the zip, John concentrated and got his energy back, all his wounds and bleeding were gone, he disappeared and reappeared in front of the Fire-eyes member who was chasing Sara and said: no one must see the nakedness of the other as lord has commanded and blew a Light bomb in the Fire-eyes face, the Fire-eyes member was thrown away and was smacked into the building but within a few seconds she reappeared in front of John and said: (in an Evil voice), we are immortal against creatures like you and punched John right in his jaw, John flew in the air but before he was smacked into the ground, the Fire-eyes member reappeared near him as she had supernatural speed and punched him again which made John to crash into the ground very hardly. The rest of the Fire-eyes members started laughing, the leader of them came forward and started kissing the female Fire-eyes member, but suddenly the ground was broken into pieces and John came out of it, he looked extremely angry and the layer of energy around him looked very bright, he looked at the female Fire-eyes member right in the face, he noticed that she was bleeding from a part of her mouth, which made him to realize that the female fire-eyes member was now connected into the air and also everything around her which made her not immunized, he then smiled and said: kiss as much as you can for there are your last kisses, then he disappeared and reappeared in front of the Fire-eyes members and said: immortal my ass! He then punched them as hard as he could, he was moving so fast that time had become slow for him again, and at the moment that John saw a drop of blood coming out of the Fire-eyes bodies he blew Light bombs into them, he was right blood would destroy their immunity towards the things around them and ultimately would make them unprotected towards the Holy powers, so the Light bombs did work and they terminated them, the rest of the Fire-eyes members attacked him too but John terminated them in the same way, after destroying them all, he turned around to see Sara, meanwhile Sara was running towards him so when he turned Sara jump on him and started kissing him, John went in dreams again, in his mind he was singing: L is for the way you look at me, O is for the only one I see, Sara pulled her head back and smiled, she said: it is really good to have a future husband like you, John smiled and said: it is also very good to have such jumpy future wife like you too, after awhile Sara pointed towards the ground and said: hey look!, John looked down and saw that the things which were destroyed were reconstructed and the street had been covered by green grass and many flowers, John bent down and removed a flower from the ground then he brought it up and said: the blessed power may bring destruction upon Evil and whatever that man has made but the end of the day will look like this as these powers are not for Destruction, they are for Construction and Protection, then he put the flower behind Sara's ear and said: and nothing is much beautiful than you Mrs. Future Seven, Sara stepped forward, cleaned Johns cloth as it was dusty and said: how many kids do you want in future? John looked a bit amazed and then while shaking his head said: ehm we could go for 4!, Sara smiled and said: anything for you and hugged John but John losed his balance and fell on his knees, Sara screamed, held Johns hand and said: what happened Johnny what happened? And Johns stomach made a very loud noise, John looked at her and said: I guess I am out of the fuel lady!, Sara smiled and said: crazy boy!, let's go find out something to eat first before we go close and see what's happening at the Temple, John agreed by nodding his head.

At the Temple, and around it . . .

People were just worshiping the God.SED; the P.SED and Sky eyes were protecting the areas around the Temple and were looking at people very accurately.

God said: was standing with closed eyes, he then slowly lifted his hands up and the supernatural mixture was separated from the ground and while twisting moved into the Sky, the whole world was amazed, no one had ever seen such commanding power, God.SED was controlling the Water, the Fire, the Sand and the Air the four main Elements of living, many people who had still faith in the true God losed their faiths and started worshiping him, God.SED lifted his hands upper and upper and the mixture moved higher and higher until it reached into the Sky at the top of the Temple, the whole world could see it as the mixture was supernaturally bright, he then smiled and in his mind said: the last step to accomplish my mission . . .

On the street middle of the city close to the Temple . . .

The city looked like it was evacuated as people had gone to the Temple, so John and Sara were all alone and were walking towards a Fast Food shop, the place where all the meals were made by chicken only. The name of the Fast Food shop was 'Fast Relieved Chicken', John looked at Sara and started making chickens sound: bood! bood! booda! baad! baad, and he pretended like the chicken was killed, Sara started laughing and said: it is too bad that we humans slaughter them and eat them, I wish I was a Vegetarian, but I am not and I am very hungry, so they moved inside the Fast Food shop which looked like the head of a chicken from outside.

The place was constructed by chickens feathers, therefore the floor was very soft and looked very lovely, the table looked like chicken which were looking down, the chair were in round shape but were made from feathers too.

Sara removed her shoes and sat on a chair and pretended like she was ordering, John took a tray and pretended like he was a waiter, Sara looked at him and said: I don't like the foods available on your menu, get me something better, John bowed down his head and said: for sure Madam, just give some of your precious time to me and I will make you lick your fingers, Sara opened her hair as they were closed by a ribbon, her hair spread in front, she looked at John and said: make it quick, John looked like he was in dream, even the tray fell from his hand, he quickly got himself together and said: I'll be right back and disappeared, Sara was going to shout as she got scared but she controlled herself, John then appeared in the kitchen, he looked around but found nothing to eat as nothing was ready in there, while looking around to find something, he heard some noises, he looked around and realized there was a basement door in there, which he thought it was the slaughtering basement, he walked a bit closer and listened, yes some noises were coming from the basement it was like someone was asking for help, he then loudly said: Ma'am I am going to the supply room to get some things, Sara was looking out of the window into the empty shops and buildings, she just said: it's okay!.

John opened the door and he closed his nose with his fingers as a very bad smell was coming out of the place, he then switched on the light and saw several stairs, but he thought it was normal so he moved down, the basement was very dark so John wasn't able to see anything, he tried to find any light keys to switch on the light but he didn't find anything, he looked around and realized that there was a very low light on the end of the place which was coming from a hole which was in the wall, so he looked more and saw some large bags of potatoes at the end of the place so he thought the food supplies were also there, and then walked towards it.

While he was moving he heard some noises again, it was like he was middle of a crowd of people but he wasn't hearing them properly, he got scared a bit, and moved faster, and suddenly stood stunned, he heard the voice of a man, the voice was weak and the man said: help me son! help me!, he turned right but couldn't see anything, he didn't know what else to do, he then remembered a verse in the Holy Bible which said: the whole world was covered by the light of his glory, so he closed his eyes and concentrate. After a very short time he started glowing, he then opened his eyes and almost paralyzed, the place wasn't the slaughtering basement or the supply area it was the torturing chambers zone, there were so many Skulls around him, so many Skeletons, it looked like the humans were being captured in there, chained and were slaughtered to make food from them, as there were many Skeletons in the chambers which had no legs or heads or hands and other parts, John heard the voice again, he turned around and scared very much, he saw an Skeleton was chained middle of two large blades and was being sucked into the wall, he looked at the Skeleton by the Holy eyes and was totally shocked this time, he saw a male soul was locked middle of two Demons and was going into the whole which looked like a burning furnace hole, he looked around and saw many other souls were too locked and were being sucked inside, the energy layer appeared around him, he then shouted: aaa enough of these Evil creatures and a large size energy bomb was blown from his body which made the whole place to shake, when Sara felt the shaking she rushed into the kitchen and into the basement, when she reached down she couldn't believe of what she was seeing, many souls smiling were standing around John, John was glowing like Moon, John looked at the souls and said: our God is a Father of love he knows where you are going now but remember if you pray you will get connected to him and he will save you, the souls bowed their heads and without saying anything were disappeared, and then Sara switched the light on, John turned around (looking very scared) said: you scared me!, while Saras mouth was wide opened replied: are you? John smiled and said: we thought these things we heard were jokes and scary stories but they all have been real and we kept avoiding them, Sara nodded her head, John then looked at the potato bags and said: forgive me Madam, we don't have chicken today, we have just potatoes to offer you . . .

At the Temple and around it . . . .

People were worshiping the God.SED faster and louder, the mixture of the Elements looked brighter and bigger, God.SED was now glowing very much and was concentrating, he opened his eyes and said: I am the God of this world, and he sent an energy wave into the mixture, and by a bright light got connected into it just like there was a line of energy between him and the mixture, he then looked at the Evil army of his, P.SED members immediately rushed inside the Temple and came out with food and drinks of all kinds, and started sharing them among people, people blindly started eating them, they didn't pay attention that the meat they were eating was from humans and the drink was the un Holy Blood of Evil & Devil, so who ate and drank losed her mind or his mind and child or old got involved in physical activities, people were kissing each other even if wouldn't know about each other, they were dancing, singing and forgot about everything else happening around them, then God.SED laughed out loud and the Evil army also laughed out loud..

At the Fast Food shop . . .

It was almost night and darkness had covered the city but still abright light was coming from the Temple and specially the mixture,

John was sitting on a chair and Sara was putting fried potatoes in his mouth, she said: how does it feel huh? John while eating said: you ask a lot of questions, he looked at Sara and said: I can't explained it, it's beyond the imaginations, when I control it, it feels like I am controlling the whole world, I feel like I have no weight, like I can run forever, I don't know how to explain it, Sara hit him weakly and said: you lucky boy! John said: blessed, you know I don't believe in luck, Sara made faces and said: ya ya you don't believe in many things, she then asked: how do you think it will be? John doubtfully said: you mean the Judgment Day? She nodded her head, John said: well it will be like the way it is written in the Holy Books perhaps, but I can feel it, it will happen sooner than we think, while he was talking, God.SED, Shouted at the Temple and said: the time has come and he lifted his hands towards the mixture and the slowly pulled them down, the mixture moved through him slowly slowly, but no one was paying attention, people were dancing, kissing, drinking and having fun, every time that the mixture got closer the land around shook, which made John and Sara to realize that something big was going on at the Temple, John hugged Sara and said: how fast do you wanna go there? Sara was going to ask what? And John disappeared and with her reappeared in front of the crowd, very close to the Temples gate. They were both shocked as the place looked like a big Party Club, a woman came to John and said: look at these baby and she removed her cloth up and showed to John her breasts, Sara moved in front of John and said: he is mine back off, John bent his head and said: you are a Lioness but cant you see that they are not normal? Sara looked around but saw nothing very strange, and said: not really they are just horny people and trying to have fun!, John remembered that he could see the truth only, he looked around and saw, many Souls, trapped by Demons which were controlling them, while John was looking Sara felt thirsty, even though she drank a lot at the Fast Food shop but unusually she felt thirsty and took a cup from one of the P.SED members tray, the P.SED member didn't recognized them as they were still wearing the P.SED cloths that they had taken, and then losed her mind and started dancing, John was looking at the mixture and knew that God.SED was going to get all the powers of the world by the things he was doing and suddenly got kissed by Sara, while being kissed said: hey! Hey!, this is no time for doing it, and the land shook again, John look at God.SED and saw he was swallowing the mixture and in a short time, he swallowed all of it and a very strong Earth Quake shook the land, God.SED laughed and said: it is done, and now I have the power of the world, and his Evil army roared and they all transformed into their true images and shapes, even God.SED transformed into Evil and Devil and they all started roaring but no one was paying attention to these activities, it was like people were all blind and couldn't hear as well, John looked at Sara and saw she was being hold by a Demon, he got angry and shouted: oh! Sara what is with you? What happened to your faith? For Christ sake! He then closed his eyes and blew the biggest energy wave that he could, the Holy energy wave acted like a huge bomb but didn't destroy anything instead it just terminated most of the Demons around the area, by doing this he acted like Flash Light middle of Darkness, and a waking call to all the people, for a moment there was no noise, no movement but then it was all screaming and running, as people started seeing the truth and real images of the Evil creatures, Evil immediately roared, several Demons came out of the Temple and rushed towards the humans, Sara started crying and said: what is with me John? (John looked angry and very serious), he looked at Sara and said: there is nothing wrong with you it's just your weak faith that puts you in trouble all the time, why can't you understand of how serious these mistakes are . . . and he heard his name

John . . . John . . . he looked towards the Temple and saw Evil was calling his name, Evil looked at Devil, Devil took a deep breath and unexcitedly pointed his finger towards John, John felt like he was locked, he was grabbed by someone, how much he tried to move he couldn't, Devil waved his finger forward and back and John automatically moved in air and stood in front of the gates, he then felt that he was released, Evil then looked at the people who were running this side and that side and shouted, he said: if you want to live stand quietly, and because people were really scared of him, they did as he ordered, several Demons stood around the people and did not allow anyone to runaway anymore, from up there in the Sky they looked like a big circle in which there were many people, Evil smiled and said: it hasn't been easy for us to find you my brother, John raised his voice and said: I prefer to die instead of being your brother, Evil laughed and said: well you can never die because you are an Immortal like us, and as per the prophecy you will join us and even lead our army, John shouted out loud and said: I will lead my Father's army if I have to lead any army, couple of Demons moved forward, and while they were roaring, they attacked John, John blew a energy wave from his body and terminated them, Evil clapped and said: isn't it just wonderful? You have the powers that we have!, John shouted out loud looking very angry said: my powers are nothing like yours, I have my Father's power and you have your Evil Masters, Evil and Devil both laughed, Evil while laughing said: oh! You are funny, but . . . meanwhile Sara was moving forward, she stood in front of John and said: shut up! Just shut up! I am sick and tired of hearing your nonsense, I have losed my true faith because of your tricks, my future husband will teach you a good lesson, meanwhile John tried to make her quite but he couldn't, Evil laughed louder and said; what a show!, haha future husband, then he sniffed and said: ohh! you are still a Virgin, many Demons moved forward and got close to them, John raised his voice up and said: leave her alone, this is me who you want not her, and an old man slapped him in the face, Evil started laughing out loud, John looked at the old man, the old man said: because of you we have losed all the fun, and many people agreed, John said(in a very confused way) : what are you talking about? can't you see their real image? A young boy said; oh! Fuck off! They are Aliens so they look like this, the other said: ya! True, they are Aliens so they look like this but see what you have done now? You made him angry our God and our Father; John didn't know what to do! He was shocked by hearing such nonsense, he wanted to cry out loud and shout for help, and he got another slap, this time a very attractive and young woman did it, she said: hey honey I was making money more than I ever did and you just ruined the fun, even a small boy came forward and hit him in his Penis which made him to bent down, the kid said: you suck man! Evil and Devil were crying almost, as they couldn't believe that humans were fighting for him against the truth, people had started fighting with John, while getting hit he heard a voice in his mind, the voice said: I am your Commander leader Gabriel, do not respond to any of the attacks, as our lord has said: if someone slapped you on one side of your face turn around show the other side and let him or her to slap but do not commit sin by harming anyone, meanwhile Sara came forward pushed people around and said: let's go Johnny lets show them some good time, John just looked at her and stood where he was, and people kept beating him, Sara looked at John while he was getting beaten and shouted: John what are you doing? Evil was rolling in himself and said: I haven't seen such drama in my entire long life, John was beaten to Death and was bleeding very bad, Sara rushed to him and covered him from getting hit and said: what are you doing John? Show them what you are capable of! Please and suddenly a very muscular man grabbed her from her hair and said: come here you little bitch! And started pulling her from back, John weakly turned around and looked at her, she was screaming and was being taken, John closed his eyes and the energy layer appeared around him, he healed and recovered immediately, he disappeared and reappeared in front of the muscular man and grabbed him from his neck and pulled him up, people's mouths fell down, John then slowly said: you will be taken just like that to Hall, and threw him into the crowd, by seeing such power people stood back, John held Sara's hand and pulled her up and then through his power blessed Sara which made her wounds that she got while battling with people to get healed and energy full again, a very bitter silence covered the whole place, people didn't know what to do, they weren't moving too, Evil smiled Evilly and disappeared and then reappeared in front of John and said: boow!, all the people around the place screamed and tried to run away but the demons around them were blocking their ways and also biting them, John just blinked, Evil became a bit angry and grabbed his throat and pulled him up, then laughed and said: I saw you like picking up humans, I like to pick up half human and half . . . John blew a Light bomb in Evils hand which made the hand to get cut off, Evil shouted out loud, several Demons moved forward to attack John but Evil roared at them so they stopped getting closer, he then smiled and his hand regenerated, he then looked at John who was guarding Sara, and said: impressive!, I thought you were half human and half Angel but I see now that you are a complete Angel already and the time stopped moving forward, and within a blink of eyes all the people were disappeared, it was like the whole world was evacuated and was left alone in the hand of John and Evil, Evil transformed into his human shape and said: oh! Johnny, why are we our own enemies huh? Look you have desires I have too, while he was talking John was just remembering of what that happened to Jesus Christ and the other Prophets when they were getting Tempted by Evil, so he was focusing very much, Evil said: you may desire this, a mountain of treasures appeared in front of John, John looked at him and said: this is what we humans made, which leaded us to you, and he blew a Light bomb into the mountain and destroyed it, Evil clapped and said: so true!, he (smiling) said: look Johnny I am the one you desire, John looked at him very angrily, Evil then said: okay! okay! Calm down son, see this, a man appeared in front of John, the Evil stroke him down, he died right away, and then Evil clapped and the man received his life back, he then said: have you heard of the song you give and take away?, John didn't move at all, Evil then grabbed Johns hand and appeared along with him in the space, then said: look at that Johnny! Two thought were going on in Johns mind in that time, first how was he breathing, second how much world had become dirty, he could not see the true color of the Earth anymore as the Earth looked much more darker than before, Evil said: it will be yours if you just join me, you can have it all I don't give a shit about it, I lived for long enough on this planet that now I am very bored of it, so you can have it all, John looked at him (very angrily) said: you are giving me the thing which is not yours and is my Father's, Evil made faces and said: alright you don't like this, then they both appeared on Earth again, on the same place which there were on it before. Evil looked around and said: aha! I smell that you are a Virgin too, he looked around and a bed appeared on a bed there was a very attractive and nude woman, her bottom was covered by the bed sheet but her breasts were out, she looked at John and said: come here honey, come here and hooked me up, and she removed the blanket from her body, John looked down and repeated I must not look at any ones nakedness, Evil said: are you shying or not liking it, ooo! I see you are a Gay man, the woman transformed into a nude Gay man, John looked at Evil and Evil smiled, then said: I feel like you are not human at all which you aren't, then the bed and the Gay man disappeared, John said: what else can you give me, Evil stood beside him, put his hand around his neck and said: everything,! John said: tell me, Evil said, everything that I just showed you! John said: what else? Evil said: my blessings!, John said: what else?, Evil replied: well my army, John smiled and said: what else? Evil started moving this side and that side, he didn't know what else he could give, he said: I can make you into a woman, John laughed said: what else?, Evil looked around and nervously said: well amm I can take you to my Father, John clapped and said: hooray what else? Evil said: oh! I can give you the Hell and make it yours, John laughed and said: what else huh? Evil didn't know what to say!, he said: what else do you need? John looked at him in a very serious way and said: can you give love? He said: whatever you want to give me, has been given to me and all the humans by my Father, but can you give love . . . Evil transformed into his real image and said: fuck off! And punched John in the stomach, for a minute John got unconscious, he never had such hit in his entire life, he then was thrown away and fell on the ground, Evil said; try not to stand up or I will take you down again but this time will be harder, but John stood up and the energy layer around him got wider and brighter, Evil said: this is what happens when you don't listen to me, he disappeared and reappeared in front of John, he threw a punch towards him but John escaped it, Evil was a bit shocked but this time throw the punch faster but John again escaped it, Evil moved back and said: I see your holy powers really work, now let's take a look at mine, the land shook, a very bright purple and black layers of energy appeared around Evils body, he looked at John and said: you are in trouble now, John stretched his neck a bit and said: bring it on, and they started fighting with each other, John wasn't believing the moves he was performing as he never been a trouble boy when he was a kid, and never learnt any Martial Arts in his entire life as he believed fighting wasn't the solution of all answers, so they kept hitting each others, every time John performed a new moved his energy level went higher and the energy layer around him became wider and brighter, even his speed of performing was increasing, after fighting a bit, he blew a very large Light bomb inside the Evils body which threw him far, John then loudly said: I call that the Super Bomb and suddenly the color of his energy level changed into yellow, his capabilities developed, he started being extremely powerful, but Evil appeared in front of him and said: you still have to learn a lot, he then pointed his finger towards John and released a very power full energy wave towards him, the energy wave looked like the waves of laser, it hit John and crossed from his body, for a minute John thought he was going to die, he felt like he was shot by a Bullet, he losed his balance and fell on the ground, Evil started walking towards him and said: Johnny! Johnny! Johnny!, you are still not ready to do such things, so don't do them, he them harshly pulled Johns head up and pointed his finger towards him, and got ready to realize another energy wave but suddenly they both heard the sound of Trumpet, the time went back into normal.

Everyone was shocked by seeing John and Evil, in that condition, and the sound of Trumpet was heard again.

Sara rushed towards John, while she was running, Evil roared and along with the rest of the Evil army they went back inside the Temple immediately, Sara reached herself to John who was getting recovered and hugged him, John said: Sara! Whatever was written in the scripture is becoming true, and heard a very loud sound of Trumpet; it was so loud that the whole world could hear it, John stood up while holding Sara's hand and while looking at the Sky said: Fire from Sky,

A huge explosion had happened in the Sun, and its radiations moved towards the whole Universe which also came to Earth, a huge cloud was appeared in the Sky all around the world and from inside of it a huge flame on Fire stroke the Earth from each sides of it. All the places on the Earth started burning, the forests, fields, buildings, everything even people catch on fire and started burning,

The second Trumpet was blown, John while hugging Sara said: something like a great mountain, burning with Fire was thrown into the sea,

And suddenly a huge Asteroid which was effected by the radiations of the Sun changed its way and while burning like a ball of Fire strokes the Earth and entered inside the Oceans, the stroke killed all the creatures living in the water, it made the world biggest Tsunami which in fact was the Tsunami of the blood of the water living animals, it stroke the land and covered on it, several people died immediately, cities were destroyed, lands were dislocated and were also destroyed.

The third Trumpet was blow, John while protecting Sara by his powers said: a great star fell from Heaven, blazing like a torch and fell on the third of the rivers like a torch and was called Worm Wood as it made the water bitter, at the same time a very shining Tail star which was effected by the radiations of the sun, headed towards the Earth and stroke in the Seas from which people were receiving water and because it was poisonous, the people who were drinking from its water were all poisoned and died, many people who were once the true God believers, fell on their faces and asked the real God for forgiveness.

The forth Trumpet was blown, John said: a third of Sun was struck, and a third of the Moon, and a third of the stars, so that a third of the light might be darkened, and a third of the Day might be kept from shining and likewise a third of the Night,

Sara screamed and said: I am scared John; John looked at her and said: why are you scared? Cheer! for the Lord is coming to take us with him, meanwhile a hugest automatic reaction happened in the Sun which caused of the creation of a huge explosion which terminated the functioning of the Sun, the sun losed its activity and was stopped, it looked like it sucked itself inside and was terminated, because the Sun was destroyed, the Moon losed its light, as well as the Stars, so also the light was taken from those countries which were in different parts of the world, so the whole world covered by darkness.

The fifth Trumpet was blown, John hugged Sara tighter and said: our little guests are coming to finish the unfinished business, meanwhile a Star which losed its reactive activity due to the destruction of the Sun changed its way and stroke the Earth, it was shoved in the deepest layers and reached into the center of the Earth, which led the melting and burning muds to burst out and move on the land, and because of the heat that it created the Insects burst out of the layers as well and attacked the people around the world, even some of the insects burst out of the place where people where gathered around the Temple and attacked the people, the place was being brighten by the weak light of the Temple so John could see the Insects flying around the place, he could see the true image of them, they were as the way they were described in the Holy Books, John smiled and said: it is written they were told not to harm the grass, or any green plant or any tree, but only those people who do no have the seal of God on their foreheads. They were allowed to kill them, and their torment was like the torment of a Scorpion when it stings someone. And in those days people will seek Death and will not find it, they will long to die, but Death will flee from them, while he was speaking a group of Insects and Locusts moved towards him and Sara but they suddenly changed their ways, then John said: they look exactly like the was they have been described in the Holy Bible, he said: in appearance the Locusts were like horses prepared for battle, on their heads were what looked like crowns of gold, their faces were like human faces, their hair like women's, their teeth like Lions, they had breastplates like breastplates of Iron, and the noise of their wings was like the noise of many chariots with horses rushing into the battle, they have tails and stings like Scorpions, and their power to hurt people for five months is in their tails, they have as king over them the Angel of the bottomless pit. He wanted to continue but he started looking around, people were running this side that side in the darkness, the Insects were attacking the people and stinging them on their bodies, they were crying and not knowing where to go as nothing was seeable except the Temple and John as he was glowing but no one could get close to him as they would feel burning as John was extremely holy by the power of Holy Spirit, and the whole world was getting destroyed.

The sixth Trumpet was blown, John shouted and said: this is our faith, this is our victory which we wanted to see, hundreds of thousands of farmers, poor people, the ones who have been humiliated by the rich, the ones who have been discriminated by the authorities, the one who had been forgotten by people, the one who had been violated, while holding torches which they made by burning a material around the stick rushed towards the other people and started attacking them to get them punished for the Evil deeds that they had done, John said: humans losed their faiths and believes in the truth and let it come sooner than anyone could imagine, these are the same soldier who were spoken of in the Holy Bible, the Book of Revelation chapter 8, verse 13, he put his head down and said: how did we bring this upon ourselves!?, he looked at Sara and saw she was just crying and looked very scared.

And the last and the seventh Trumpet was blown away, John whispered in the ear of Sara: there were loud voices in Heaven saying the kingdom of the world has become the kingdom of our lord and of his Christ and he shall reign forever and ever, and disappeared and while holding Sara he reappeared at the top of the pillar inside the Temple where Evil and the rest of the army where roaring.

Evil looked at him and said; this is just the beginning of what we have been waiting for, John shout and said: all these years humans enjoyed, and acted like they had no awareness regarding this truth because of you and your makers, but now is the time of reality not imaginations, and while he was speaking he felt something, he immediately looked at the Sky, there exist a light in the Sky which was difficult for anyone to look at it as it was very bright, the light covered the whole world, it looked like everywhere was morning, the white clouds appeared in the sky and from the middle of them a brighter light came out, and after looking at it, people saw a man standing who John knew he was the Holy son of God, (the Christ), his face was too shiny that no one could look at it, he then raised his right hand and the Souls of the people were separated from their biological bodies, the then souls from the animals and the Insects and all the other living creatures, several Angels came out of the clouds and flew with a very fast speed towards the Earth and started collecting the Souls which had the Holy Sign on their foreheads, Evil and the rest of the Evil army were just roaring but weren't moving to another place from the place which they were standing on it, within few seconds, the Angels collected the Souls and went back into the clouds and the man also moved back into the clouds, immediately after he went inside Gabriel came out of there and flew towards John, and stood beside him, he looked extremely muscular and powerful, he was around 190cm, he had cloths made by feathers and to very large wings, he had no hair and the color of his eyes was the mixture of brown and green.

Gabriel looked at Evil and Devil and said: non of you look like your Father, the Evil and Devil roared at him but they couldn't move as the time wasn't right for them, he then looked at John and said: let's go! And raised his hand towards him, he held Gabriel`s hand with one hand and held Saras hand with the other, and Gabriel started flying but how much John tried to pull Sara from the ground he couldn't, it was like she was stuck into the ground, Sara was looking at him and her tears were falling, Evil laughed and said: Great! Gabriel can't pick up some low weights, John looked at Gabriel and said: what`s wrong, Gabriel looked at him and said: she cannot come as she has not the Holy Sign, John immediately turned around and realized it was true, he also noticed that Sara had already become a soul as well as him but he was glowing very much, by looking at her his tears fell down, he looked at Gabriel again and said: but she was and is a good girl, even she kept her virginity for all these years, Gabriel replied, but she never had the true faith, John said: please commander I beg of you please take her with us, Gabriel looked at him in every serious was and said: John every second counts, she cannot come with us even though I personally loved her as she had been very great as a human but she cannot join us, John didn't know what to do!, he started looking like a mentally disordered person, his tears were not coming out of his eyes anymore, Evil said: ahh fuck you all with your love stories! Can't you take them up or shall we help you? And the Evil army laughed, John looked at Gabriel and said: may I have some private moment with her sir?, Gabriel looked at him and said: of course and suddenly the whole time changed, John looked around, he was inside his room and was wearing some normal cloths, Sara was standing right in front of him, they both hugged each other very tight, Sara said; why? Why Now huh? Tell me why? John looked at her and said: we have been warned for thousands of years, we knew some day like this would come, Sara said: its okay you promised me that you wont leave me alone so it doesn't matter what happens next!, John separated himself from her very gently and said: I have to go, Sara said: what? How can you leave me like this? You promised me John? What will I do without you?

John put his hands on her shoulders and said: everything will be alright, he said; as per the scripture, the war, will start very soon, so when I come back I will . . . Sara shouted said: I hate you Mr. Seven I hate you, it would be better if you would go to Hell, John smiled and said: you don't mean that right? Sara pushed him back and said: I mean it, why you have to be the best every time? John looked at her very confused and said: what are you talking about? Sara shouted said: enough of acting like you don't know anything, you were always the best in everything, you were best in class, best in sport, best in learning and doing things, and now an Angel who is the chosen one and the best, why you? Why you huh? I did everything you told me to, I went with you to church at all times, I did everything that I could but you were always the best and no one ever recognized me and recognizes me. John couldn't believe of what he was hearing, very angrily he replied: what are you crazy? I certainly know that it will be unimaginable living with those Monsters out there for some times but how can I protect you more than this while I have not yet transformed into a complete Angel huh? Sara please look at me when I am talking to you!, ah Jesus Christ, I have no choice, I have to go, I know you . . . . . Please Sara! I just ammm, Sara turned around and looked at him in the face, she walked forward and said: will you promise me that you will come back for me? John smiled and said: I promise, she said; you broke your promise once don't repeat it again, and started crying, John hugged her very tightly and said: I am sorry! I know staying in this place will have its own risks and dangers but if I don't go, we can never be protected, Sara looked at him and said: your love for father is beyond imaginations, you can even leave me to fulfill what father has planned for you, I wish you had this much love for me, now kiss your future wife for the last time, John looked at her and said: this kiss isn't the last one, it's the first one of the new life, and they started kissing and appeared back on the pillar, Gabriel said: are you ready Johanna? John looked at him and then whispered something in his ear, he said: please bless her send her away from this place after we go and let her have safety by staying in some safe place, Gabriel replied: as you are the chosen one I accept your request, and Sara started getting invisible, she tried to cry but had no more tears as she wasn't a human anymore, but Johns tears kept falling down, Sara waved her hand and disappeared, after she went John couldn't control himself, he looked at Evil and his army and said: soon! Soon! I will come back to finish our unfinished business and started being pulled up by Gabriel, while he was going up. Devil shouted said: I will make her my wife until you come back pussy! And they laughed . . .

The new Heaven and New Earth . . .

A male young Angel said: then what happened?, John smiled and said: it was just the beginning of the new end . . .

To be continued . . .

With Respect

John [illegible]